BLEAKWOOD LORE

The Blacksmith Legacy: Addendum One

BEN IRELAND

Ireland,
INK

Library of Congress
2 0 1 9 9 0 3 4 1 7

BISAC: Young Adult/Urban Fantasy/Monsters/Adventure/Humor/Friendship
Paperback:
ISBN-13: 978-1-7335011-0-1
ISBN-10: 1-7335011-0-X

I dedicate this to myself.
Ben, I wouldn't be the man I am today without you.

Other Books by Ben Ireland

Young Adult Fantasy

The Blacksmith Legacy

Billy Blacksmith: The Demonslayer

Billy Blacksmith: The Hellforged

Billy Blacksmith: The Ironsoul

Urban Fantasy/Cyberhorror

The Kingdom City Series

Resurrection

Revolt

Retribution *(forthcoming)*

Short stories

A Dash of Madness

Kissed A Snake

Moments In Millennia

Fairykin

Sanguification

BLEAKWOOD LORE

Table øf Cøntents

SPIDERS

25ft

20ft

15ft

10ft

5ft

TREMANCHEN
8-10ft

BILLY
6ft 4in

SHADOW LURK
5ft

SCULNEP
2ft

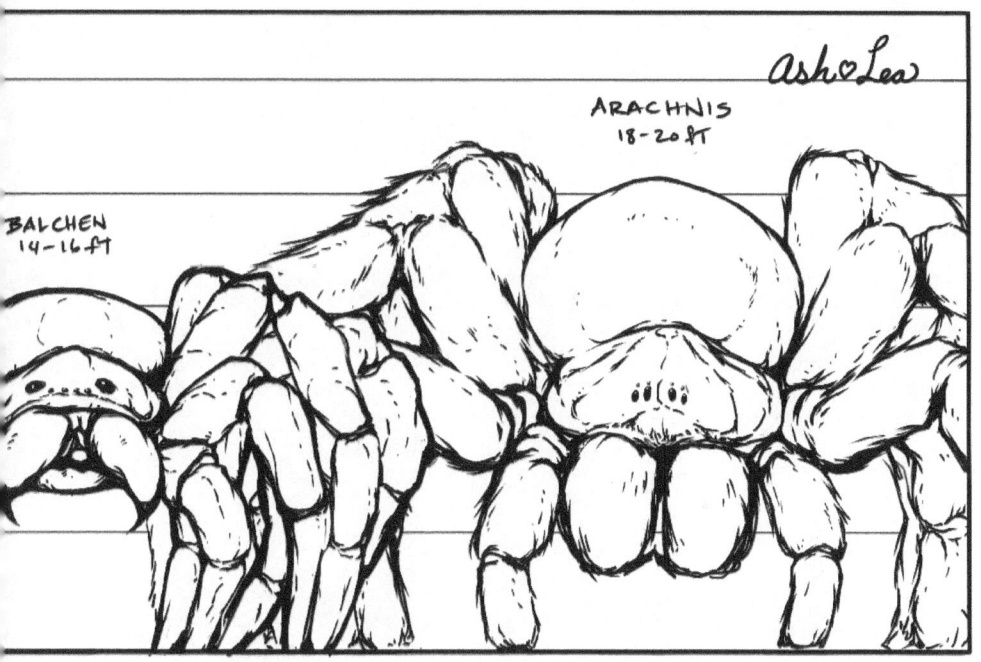

Minør
League Demønslayers

THREE MONTHS PRIOR TO THE WELL

Six members of the Sugar House Wasp minor league baseball team were already seated when Christopher Blacksmith walked in to the Salty Dragon on a blustery, cold October evening. His teammates raised their glasses at the sight of him and gave a warm, slightly wet, welcoming cheer that made Chris smile. He'd been a Sugar House Wasp for only a few months now, but they already felt like family. He bet they'd been through a lot more than most minor league teams ever would.

The bar was a cozy, amber colored room, set in the corner of a strip mall on the outskirts of Sugar House, a city just north of Bleakwood. The furnishings were made out of wood, the stained-glass light fixtures casting the bar in an array of muted hues. A huge TV hung in the corner, playing game one of the World Series. The patrons were all in their young twenties, wearing fancy jackets that Chris could never afford, every other head dyed a different shade of the rainbow. Mostly college kids relaxing after a hard Thursday.

Ember Ascua sat at a table on the far side of the room, facing the door. She was beautiful and athletic, with deep skin, her dark hair flowing from under her grey Sugar House Wasp cap. She had a good heart, but took too many things seriously, in Chris' opinion—even drinking. She rose as Chris walked in and snatched a chair from the nearest table without a 'do you mind?' to the group sitting there.

"Christopher," Ember called, holding her beer bottle high. "Bienvenidos."

"Hey," Chris said to the table at large. He sat down next to Crystal Glass, a tall girl with round cheeks, short blonde hair, and kind blue eyes. She fiddled with a cup of water on the table and flashed Chris a nervous smile. She didn't usually join the team at the bar, but this time it was important.

The fraternal twins, Kelly and Ivy Green sat across from him, sipping on mugs of beer and building a log cabin with their order of fries. They looked identical, same brown hair, same brown eyes, but Kelly's hair was short, and Ivy's hair was long. Kelly had been a paramedic since just after high school. He was exactly the kind of guy to have on your team in situations like this. Ivy was a registered nurse and always carried a bag of equipment she may, or may not, have been allowed to remove from the hospital. Other than saving lives, they didn't take anything seriously, even baseball. But they were insanely good at baseball anyway.

"Batter up," Kelly called as he pitched a fry at Chris.

The fry zipped over the table. Chris snatched it out of the air and popped it into his mouth. Beaming, he waved on an invisible crowd as they cheered for him.

"Strike!" Ivy shouted, and they laughed.

Next to the twins sat Beryl Azure, she went by the name Bee. She was a big person, hands down the biggest individual on the team. She was probably as big as Chris' brother Billy, but in better shape, with sinuous tendons rippling in her forearms as she picked up a jalapeno popper and bit into it. Her head was shaved, her dark skin reflecting the bar lights.

Bee sat next to Auburn Fawn, a pale girl with copious curls of red hair, who was laughing at whatever Bee had just said. She was a decent baseball player, but what she had going for her was her speed. She didn't have to hit the ball very hard and she was already at the next base. That, and she could read the opposing team like a book. Not much got by Fawn, but if it did, she caught up, fast.

"Holla at ya girl, Stick," Bee said, calling Chris by the name she'd picked out for him. Bee had a thing for nicknames.

"Did you get it?" Auburn asked in her smoky, low voice. Chris couldn't help smiling every time she spoke.

"I did," Chris announced proudly.

The table hushed, the log cabin construction ceasing temporarily. Chris slipped out of his backpack and placed it on his chair. Zipping it open, he withdrew the thermal imager. The device had a screen about the size of a smartphone on it, but with a thick handle on the bottom so you could aim it like a ray gun.

"That going to do the trick?" Ember asked skeptically, her face serious.

"Guess we'll find out," Chris replied.

Crystal sipped on her water, her hand shaking. "So it sees through walls?" she asked, squeezing her eyes shut awkwardly, as if speaking had physically hurt her. She usually looked embarrassed when she said anything. The only time she didn't seem self-conscious was on the baseball field.

"It detects heat," Chris explained. "If there is a body in there, and it's hot, we should be able to see it. Look."

Chris flipped on the imager and passed it around the table. Crystal let out an 'ooo' as she aimed it at the twins. They put their arms around each other and waved at her. She passed it on, each person taking a minute to point the imager around the room, at the lights, at the fireplace in the corner, at the ducts in the ceiling.

"Careful with that," Chris said, resisting the urge to snatch it out of Ember's hands. "It costs more than two thousand dollars. I'm toast if my boss finds out I took it."

"Two grand?" Bee let out a low whistle. "Might have to forget to give it back." She laughed.

Chris chuckled, trying very hard to make the smile on his face look genuine.

"You know the plan?" Ember said to the table at large, grinding her right fist into the palm of her left hand. "Let's do this."

"I just got here," Chris complained. "Can't I eat first?"

"I work early, Stick," Bee said. "The sooner the better for me."

"I . . ." Crystal swallowed. "I just want to get it over with."

Ember thrust the imager at him and picked up her coat. Chris groaned and slipped the device into his backpack.

"Fine," Chris said. "Kelly, hit me up with some fries. I can't do this hungry."

Kelly slid the plate across the table and stood. Everyone stood. *Ugh. I'm too hungry for this,* Chris thought as he stuffed a handful of fries in his mouth. He followed the team out into the chilly night air. It wasn't snowing in the valley just yet, but the snow-covered tops of the mountain painted an icy blue silhouette in the moonlight.

"Should we carpool?" Chris asked. "Save some gas."

"I'm already with Bee," Auburn said as she zipped her coat and climbed up into Bee's huge Ford F-250.

"Our back seat is covered in boxes," Ivy said as she climbed into the driver's seat of her forest green Subaru Outback, and her brother climbed into the passenger side. "Sorry."

"I'll ride with you." Ember nodded in Chris' direction.

I meant save me gas, Chris mused. "Sounds good."

He didn't want to drive alone, anyway. Not where they were going.

"Crystal," Ember called. Crystal let out a peep and turned. She was already most of the way across the parking lot. "Ride with us."

"Oh. Okay." Crystal started back toward them, her hands stuffed deep into her coat pockets, her eyes on her shoes. She arrived at Chris' truck and didn't seem to know what to do next.

Ember opened the door for her. "Get in," she instructed.

Crystal climbed in and Ember jumped in behind her.

Tucked in the front seat of his ancient Ford truck, with Crystal in the middle and Ember by the window, Chris pulled into the street. Ember drew her baseball bat out of her bag and rested it between her feet, turning it back and forth slowly. Crystal pressed her hands between her knees, like she was trying to be as small as possible.

"Tell him where to go," Ember said.

"Head towards Bleakwood," Crystal whispered. "It's on Industrial Court. Behind the steel factory."

"Okay." Chris took a deep breath. This was it. They had been tracking them down for months, and it seemed like they were finally going to find them.

Chris didn't want to find them. If he was lucky, the team would see the eight-legged heat blobs through the wall and run. He glanced across the cab at Ember; her face steel-hard and determined. She wasn't going to quit. She never did. It made her a good minor league captain. But this was so much more serious than baseball.

"What makes you think they're there?" Ember asked, her gaze out the window, tracing the buildings as they passed.

"My uncle found them yesterday in his barn," Crystal said. "He thinks he shot one, but they all ran. He followed them and saw them disappear around here. That's the only warehouse on the block that's empty. Nobody has been in there for years. He checked it out today and said he could see them crawling around in there."

"Why did he tell you instead of calling the police?" Chris asked.

"He did call the police," Crystal explained. "They laughed at him. He kind of has a reputation already, so they weren't willing to listen."

"It fits with what we've found," Chris said. "They were moving towards the mountains until they ran into your uncle."

17

"Why don't they just go there already?" Ember asked, bouncing her bat off the floor of the cab. "It's been weeks and they're moving no more than a few streets at a time. Why don't they just make a run for it?"

Chris glanced out the window at the mountains looming over the weathered, wooden *Welcome to Bleakwood* sign. "Maybe they don't like the cold. Those mountains already have snow on them."

"I bet they're sick," Crystal said. "There probably isn't any demon food for them over here."

"Nah." Ember tapped the floor with her bat. "They eat people. Plenty of people around here."

The car was stuffed to the roof with a thick silence for the remainder of the short drive. It made Chris' neck itch. The last thing he wanted to do was go hunting for trouble, but there were two reasons why he couldn't sit back at the Salty Dragon and let the rest of the team get themselves killed.

First of all, it was his fault they were in this mess in the first place. If he'd just kept his mouth shut when someone mentioned the spiders, they wouldn't have started hunting them. But he was glad to have someone to talk to about the insane things happening. He tried to leave Billy alone; that poor kid had more than enough on his plate. So when the team started talking about spiders and *not* laughing at him, he couldn't stop himself from spilling the beans.

Second of all, he couldn't let these guys go alone. They needed help, and darn it, Chris couldn't help himself when someone was in need. If what they were trying to do was made easier because he was there, nothing was going to stop him from being there. Not even knee-shaking terror and a constant urge to fear-puke.

Finally, Crystal pointed to a cluster of dark warehouses to their right. "This is it," she whispered.

Chris turned into the parking lot and Ember reached across and flipped off the headlights.

"Hey," Chris protested.

"Don't want them to know we're here," Ember said.

"They're going to hear the cars," Chris muttered, stopping his truck in the middle of the parking lot before he drove into something he couldn't see.

The other Wasps pulled into the parking lot behind them. The area was dusty, with tufts of grass growing in cracks between the slabs of cement. A tree in front of the building was breaking out of the brick wall surrounding it, tall blades of grass brushing the windowsill behind it. The warehouse looked almost like any other on the street, like an oversized tool shed; a story and a half tall, three hundred yards long, fifty yards wide, all made of corrugated iron. The only difference was this building didn't have an illuminated marquee over the door.

Chris' eyes fell on the webs hanging from the awning above the entrance, blowing in the breeze like party streamers. "They're here."

Everyone started climbing out, their Sugar House Wasp coats zipped up to their necks, their baseball bats in their hands. Chris took a deep breath and joined them. The wind cut through his thin t-shirt and he slipped into his jacket.

"How do ya'll want to do this?" Bee asked the group.

"Chris." Ember pointed to a broken down, chain-link fence on the right side of the building. "Walk around the building with your heat detector and see if you can find any inside."

"What? Alone?" Chris asked.

"Naw," Bee said. "If you can see them, I want to know about it. I'm going with you."

"I'm sticking with Bee." Fawn hugged Bee around her arm. Bee made a face like Fawn was invading her personal space, but she didn't complain.

"Ditto," Kelly and Ivy declared in unison.

"Alright," Ember said. "I'll wait out here with Crystal. See if any come through the door."

"O—oh," Crystal said in a small voice.

Chris walked to the bed of his truck and pulled the heat detector and his bat out of his bag. "Let's go."

He trudged around to the side of the building, stepping over the twisted remains of the fence which looked like someone had driven through it at some point. Bee, Kelly, Ivy, and Fawn followed, huddled close behind.

The wind blew constantly, rustling the trees that lined the property. That was a mercy, since anything inside the building probably couldn't hear their chorus of stomping footsteps.

Chris pointed the detector at the side of the warehouse and flipped it on. The screen showed a solid blur of dark blue where the corrugated iron wall stood in front of them.

"What do you see?" Kelly asked.

"Nothing," Chris said. "It's a huge, cold metal wall." He started pacing to his right, holding up the heat detector. "We're not going to be able to see anything from this."

Kelly and Ivy pressed into his sides, while Bee looked over his shoulder at the screen.

"It ain't working," Bee said.

Chris pointed the screen at Kelly's chest. He held his arms out wide as the screen lit up with a blur of red.

He pointed it back at the wall and kept walking. The wall slid past them, an unyielding barrier of blue. A sudden gush of wind pushed Chris back a step as a loud snap sounded behind him. Chris let out an embarrassing yelp of surprise. Fortunately, it was covered by Ivy and Kelly's much louder shriek.

"What the heck?" Chris exclaimed.

"What was that?" Fawn asked, gripping Bee's arm harder.

"Did anyone bring a flashlight?" Chris asked.

Nobody had.

"Ya'll suck at this," Bee said. "Going monster hunting and nobody brings a flashlight?"

Bee walked towards the darkness and picked a branch that had been blown off a tree by the wind. She held it up by way of illustration then tossed it to the ground.

"What about my phone?" Fawn asked.

"Nobody light up anything, yet," Chris said. "We don't want to give away our position."

Bee scoffed. "I'm sure they can hear ya'll squealing just fine."

Chris shook the heat detector in annoyance. "This isn't going to do us any good. It's not the right kind to see through solid metal."

"What about a window?" Fawn asked, pointing to a small square of glass high in the wall.

Chris nodded. "That would work."

"Except nobody can reach it," Ivy pointed out.

"We could form a human pyramid," Kelly suggested.

"I could climb on Bee's shoulders," Fawn said, grabbing at her hair as it blew about her face in the wind.

Bee's eyes widened as she stared down the group. "Nobody is climbing on me."

"There are pallets." Ivy pointed to several squares of old-looking wood scattered around the yard. "We could stack them. It might give Bee enough height to reach the window."

"That works," Kelly said. "Race ya." He dashed off into the night as Ivy sprinted the other direction. Moments later, Ivy emerged from the shadows, dragging a large wooden pallet over the grass. Everyone followed suit, grabbing the discarded pallets and stacking them under the window.

When they were done, the uneven pile of wooden pallets was stacked six feet high.

"Well, that looks unsafe," Kelly observed.

"Ivy," Bee said. "You get up there, you're the smallest. Less likely to collapse under you."

"Sure, but I couldn't reach the window."

Bee looked around the group, then grumbled in frustration. "Man, ya'll lucky you got me to come along on this expedition. Ya'll'd be lost without me." She started climbing the pallets, which rocked under her weight. "I ain't no dainty flower. You know how much weight I got on me? Climbing on stacks of wood like a kid—" she stopped talking as the stack let out a huge crack and sunk several inches.

"You okay?" Chris asked.

"Ya'll better catch me," she said, placing a hand on the warehouse wall to steady herself. She rose slowly. "This isn't going to work," she said, looking squarely at the steel before her.

"Can you reach the window?" Ivy asked.

Bee reached her hand up and wiggled her fingers in front of the glass.

Fawn clapped in excitement. "Awesome."

"Take this," Chris said.

Chris reached up and handed Bee the heat detector. Bee raised it slowly above her head, trying to not unbalance the wobbling pile of wood under her. She pointed it through the window.

"I cain't see nothing," Bee said. "This is really great. Got me standing on a stack of blocks like an idiot."

"Wait," Chris said. He walked backwards, until he could see the screen in Bee's hand. "Keep it steady."

"Steady? I'm getting ready to break my ass and you want me to be steady?"

Kelly, Ivy, and Fawn trotted back to stand next to Chris.

"No, we can see the screen," Fawn said. "You're doing great."

"Slide it across the floor," Ivy said.

Bee twisted her hand. Despite her complaining, she was strong and in control over her body, and the image on the small display panned across the floor of the warehouse. The cavernous room showed up as blips of blue and grey on the tiny screen.

"I can't see anything," Kelly whispered.

"Keep going," Ivy said.

"WAIT," they all chorused at once.

A small spot of red had appeared on the display. Chris couldn't tell what it was. It could have been a metal barrel still hot from the sun through a window. It could have been a demon spider.

"The screen is too far away," Fawn said.

"Did it move?" Kelly asked. "I think it just moved."

"That was me," Bee said. "I'm going to drop all two grand of this damn thing if I have to stand up here much longer."

But it really looked like it moved. Maybe. It was just a small speck of red on a tiny screen being held ten feet up in the air. There was simply no way to tell.

Then it did move.

The spot of light suddenly grew bigger, growing as whatever on the other side of the window raced towards them, gripping the ceiling as it came.

Ivy screamed.

"Go," Chris shouted.

Something slammed into the wall of the warehouse, shaking the corrugated iron up and down the length of the building. Bee let out a low shout of surprise, and the pallets under her rocked violently. A set of milky, pink eyes the size of tennis balls peered through the window from a hairy face. Chris prayed it was too dark for the thing to see anything, but he wasn't going to take any chances. He bolted, following Ivy and Kelly as they raced back towards the chain-link fence. He glanced over his shoulder, then stopped, his shoes slipping on the grass. Fawn was the only one that had stayed behind to help Bee. The pallets tipped as Bee turned, and she fell on to her back, sliding forward as the pallets tumbled over Fawn. Chris gasped, fearing Fawn had been crushed, but seconds later, Bee was pulling Fawn to her feet and they ran.

"The hell was that?" Bee shouted as she bolted past Chris.

Fawn caught up, running, but her steps were unsteady. Chris put his shoulder under her arm and helped her move, her limp growing with each step.

Fawn was trying to be tough. She was a great baseball player, skilled and competitive, and always the sportswoman. She didn't let little injuries bother her either. But Chris could hear her breathing growing more labored each second. By the time they were in the parking lot, she couldn't even put weight on her left leg, letting out soft whimpers as she moved.

"What happened?" Ember asked, striding up to them, scanning Fawn from head to toe.

"We saw something in there," he said.

"I got that already," Ember replied. "Fawn, you okay?"

Fawn shook her head, her lips pressed together too tightly to respond.

Chris helped her limp over to Bee's truck and sat her down the running board. Fawn gripped her knee, hissing in pain.

"Oh, my," Crystal said in a shaking voice.

The group started murmuring in shock before Chris could step back and see.

Fawn's lower leg was soaked in blood. Her jeans had been torn away by the pallets, and Chris could see two deep gouges, like nails protruding from the wood had dug into her just below the knee, and rode all the way down her calf muscle.

"Aw spit, girl," Bee said. "We got to get you to a hospital, and I have a strict no-bleeding policy in my truck."

Fawn grabbed her knee above the wound and squeezed, leaning forward as she let out a whine, then a high moan of pain.

"I guess I can make an exception," Bee said. "You guys got a first aid kid?"

Kelly and Ivy had already sprung into action. Kelly was racing back from his car with a large canvas bag in his hand.

"Let's lie you down in the truck," Ivy said.

Bee lifted Fawn and lay her down in the bed of the truck. Ivy climbed in after her.

"What can I do to help?" Chris asked.

"Keep an eye out to see if anything followed us." Kelly zipped open the bag and pulled out a roll of bandages and a tube of some kind of medicine. He handed the bandages to Ivy. He rolled Fawn onto her side and started wiping the wounds with a cloth.

Fawn screamed, then stuffed her hand in her mouth to muffle the sound.

"We'll get you patched up," Ivy said as she inspected the injury. "But you need to get those cleaned out and stitched up."

"When was your last tetanus shot?" Kelly asked.

Fawn shook her head, unsure. Kelly squirted the goo onto Fawn's leg, and Ivy began binding it with quick, practiced motions.

"It's a good thing we got two EMTs on the team," Ember said. She was watching the building, her bat raised defensively.

"I'm a paramedic," Kelly said.

"I'm an RN," Ivy added.

Bee looked between them. "What's the difference?"

"One stops you from dying," Kelly said, holding the bandage in place as Ivy worked.

"The other keeps you alive," Ivy explained.

"Fawn," Ivy patted her shoulder. "You're going to be okay. And on the plus side, you're going to have a bad-ass scar."

"Yay," Fawn wheezed.

Fawn scooted to the end of the truck where Bee picked her up. She rested her head against Bee's shoulder, her eyes pressed closed as she stifled sounds of agony. Fawn looked tiny in Bee's arms.

"You guys go," Ember said. "We'll take it from here, Fawn. You did great."

"I didn't actually do anything," Fawn said between clenched teeth.

Chris ran around the passenger side and opened the door. Bee followed and set her in the passenger seat. In the cab lights of the truck, Chris could see blood pulsing through the bandage, seeping into her sock and shoe.

Chris patted her shoulder. "You'll be okay."

Fawn let her head fall back and nodded without opening her eyes. She let out another moan of pain as Chris closed the door.

The Wasps stood together, watching with growing dismay as their strongest hitter drove away.

"Maybe we should come back later," Crystal said. "We need Bee for this."

"No," Ember insisted. "We know something is in there. It knows we're out here. If we don't go now they're going to get away again."

"Why *did* we just let Bee leave?" Chris asked. "I could have taken Fawn."

"Come on," Kelly said, his eyes fixed on the warehouse. "Let's do this. They're going to hurt someone if we don't stop them."

Ember swung her bat in a circle with one hand and started towards the front door. "I'm doing it myself if I have to."

That kind of attitude made her a good leader, but Chris wasn't sure if it translated into spider hunting. Chris followed Ember, standing shoulder to shoulder with Ivy and Kelly as they walked. It took a few seconds but then he heard Crystal following behind them. They reached the door nestled under a small tin awning. It was a common door made of glass, with a chain hanging through the door handles. But a long gouge ran through the glass and metal frame, as if thick, sharp claws had dug into it as something tried to force the doors open. Chris paused, contemplating the size of those claw marks.

Ember nudged him aside as she reached into her coat and pulled out a pair of bolt cutters. She handed her bat to Chris. The bolt cutters bit into the chain, and Ember forced down with both hands, slowly prying the metal apart. As Ember gave a grunt of effort, the chain finally snapped and slid to the ground with a bang.

Kelly flinched. "Geesh."

"You have to be quieter," Ivy hissed.

"Then next time catch the freaking chain," Ember spat. She pulled on the door, but it didn't budge. "Damn, it's locked."

"I've got this." Crystal stepped forward and knelt in front of the door. She pulled a small leather wallet out of her pocket, placed it on her knee and flipped it open. Inside lay small metal tools Chris recognized as lock picks.

"Nice," Kelly said. "You're always a surprise, Crystal."

"Don't congratulate me yet." She picked two tools from the wallet and slid them into the lock.

"Do you always have lock picks in your pocket?" Chris asked.

"Shh," Crystal responded. Three seconds later, the lock slipped open with a snap.

"Now can we congratulate you?" Kelly asked.

Crystal gave a shaking smile and slipped the wallet back into her jeans.

Chris couldn't stop staring at Crystal. *Where did a girl like that learn to pick locks?* he thought.

Ember put her hand on the door handle but paused. "Okay, you ready? We don't know what is waiting in there for us. Or how many. But we need to make this count. There are people in this city that are counting on us that don't know it."

An explosive crash sounded from just beyond the door; like someone had violently upended grandma's favorite china cabinet.

Ember jumped back. "What the hell was that?"

For the first time that night Chris saw a hint of uncertainty in Ember's eyes. Chris' heart was in his throat. The last thing he wanted to do was walk into whatever the hell would make a noise like that.

Crystal paced backwards three yards before she stopped. "I don't think we should go in there."

And just like that, Ember's uncertainty was gone. She pulled on the handle, and a warm gust of air blew past Chris. The days were still sunny enough to heat up the tin building. Chris took the door, letting Ember, Kelly, Ivy, and Crystal in first. *I am a gentleman, after all*, he thought.

The lobby of the building was small and dusty, a table pushed up against the wall to their right, under a blind-covered window. The floor was carpeted in broken glass. Though there were no busted windows, almost like someone had dumped out a huge box of beer bottles all over the floor. A single door in the far wall opened into a shadowy abyss.

Crystal muttered what sounded like a prayer under her breath. "What are we planning here?"

Kelly stepped protectively in front of his sister. "We don't know what's in there."

"Where is the heat detector?" Ivy asked.

Chris felt his stomach drop. "I don't know. I think Bee dropped it when she fell."

"We . . . we should go," Crystal urged.

"No." Ember strode towards the door and into the darkness beyond.

Crystal let out a peep. Kelly and Ivy held up their bats. Chris' mouth fell open.

"Keep up," Ember hissed from the shadows.

Chris stepped forward, following the group into the warehouse. The room was huge, the roof and far wall swallowed in gloom. A single window high up on the wall to their right let in shifting rays of light, tossed about by the trees blowing in the wind. That must have been the window through which they'd seen the spider. But there was no sign of the monster now. As far as he could tell the warehouse was empty.

"Stay together," Ember whispered as she walked.

Kelly, Ivy, and Crystal trotted up behind Ember. Chris moved more slowly. Not just because of the fear making it hard to move his feet, but he never liked rushing into things. Not like Ember did. He preferred to look around. Being able to see would be a huge benefit in a situation like this. Plus if he found the heat detector before it started raining on it, he might not get fired.

Something brushed the side of Chris' shoe and he looked down. Some metal object at his feet reflected dimly in the low light. He stooped and picked it up. It was a dog collar. There was a pile of at least thirty of them right by the door. His stomach twisted, threatening to eject the french-fries at what that meant.

A thought occurred to him and Chris stood abruptly, facing the door. If he was a giant spider luring idiots into a trap, the place he'd choose to hide is directly above the door said idiots would walk in through.

He traced the wall above the entrance, thankfully not seeing any huge sets of eyes staring back at him. But something he did notice was a small string attached to the door, right at the top. It was oddly placed in the corner and bent around the frame heading directly for the ceiling. For some reason reminded Chris of a draw bridge rope. He reached up and touched it. The string stuck to his finger. It was sticky—like spiderweb.

Something yanked on the string and the door slammed closed. Chris spun around to see the group frozen in shock from the noise. The light from the window flashed white as the headlights of a passing vehicle illuminated the ceiling momentarily. Directly above them, bound in thick ropes of web, a forklift had been suspended.

"Hey," was all Chris managed to shout as without a sound, the forklift dropped.

Kelly glanced up and saw what Chris had. He grabbed Crystal, Ivy, and Ember the best he could, and tackled them, shoving them out of the way as the forklift crashed into the ground behind them.

Kelly managed to avoid being crushed, but part of the frame cracked off the forklift as it crashed into the floor, whacking him in the back. He slammed face-first into the cement.

"Kelly," Ivy shouted as she crawled over to him.

29

Crystal and Ember sat up, too dazed by what had just happened to hear the creaking that echoed through the warehouse. Chris looked around, unable to see what was making the ominous grating sound.

"Move," Chris shouted.

Barely illuminated in the faint light, the wall of the warehouse appeared to tilt forward. It took a second for Chris to realize that some*thing* had lined up dozens of long, heavy pipes against the wall and had just let them loose. They fell like two dozen axes, dropping towards Crystal, Ember, Ivy, and Kelly.

Ember jumped to her feet and grabbed Kelly, dragging him by the back of his shirt. Crystal only had time to look up and register what was happening. She rolled over, putting her chest over Ivy's head. She screamed as the pipes struck.

The clangor of the pipes hitting the cement was enormous, drowning out the sound of the wind outside. They clatter and clanged for more than a minute, bouncing off the cement and rolling all over the place.

Chris ran towards his friends as the ringing echoed into silence. Ember sat behind the demolished forklift, panting, Kelly lay next to her, blinking dazed eyes. Chris ran up to Crystal and began hefting the pipes off her. They were heavy things, at least twenty feet long. If it hadn't been for Crystal's thick jersey, they probably would have cut her. She was going to be nothing but bruises under there. She whimpered as Chris moved the pipes.

"You okay?" Chris asked.

Crystal shook her head. She rolled over and Chris got a good look at Ivy. She was out cold.

"I'm sorry," Crystal panted. "I tried to protect her, but I think she hit her head."

"That's okay," Chris said. He glanced up at Crystal to give her a reassuring smile but felt the smile disappear as he saw how much blood ran from under her hair.

"What is it?' Crystal asked.

"Nothing. Just need you to stay right here with Ivy, okay? Take care of her." Chris grabbed Ivy by her shoulders and dragged her behind the forklift.

Crystal nodded and crawled over to Ivy, sitting against the forklift and resting Ivy's head on her lap. She brushed the hair from Ivy's face, her own breathing hard and shaking.

"Ivy." Chris knelt next to her and patted her cheek. They were going to have to get her out of here if she didn't wake up. Unfortunately she woke up.

"My head hurts," she said.

"How many fingers am I holding up?" Chris asked, holding up three fingers.

"One for each brain cell in your head," Ivy replied.

"Seriously," Chris said.

"I am being serious. Three."

He slipped Ivy's baseball bat back into her hand. "I think there is something in here. As soon as you can stand, get to the door."

Ivy gave a weak smile and nodded. "Yeah, I think there is something in here too. Glad we can agree."

"How are you?" Chris leaned over and whispered to Ember.

"I'm pissed, thanks for asking." She flexed her arms to make sure they still worked.

"Something is in here and it's trying to kill us," Chris whispered.

Ember gave him a flat look. "I noticed."

"We need to leave. We're not ready for this," Chris said. "I don't know how bad Ivy is hurt."

"Like hell I'm leaving," Ember replied. She picked up her baseball bat and stood.

"Kelly, you okay?"

Kelly shook his head. He pulled himself up next to Crystal. "My back. Forklift hit it pretty hard."

"Broken?" Chris asked.

"Totally," Kelly wheezed. "The forklift fell at least twenty feet. It's completely trashed."

Chris blinked.

"My back's fine," Kelly said. "Might need a few weeks off, though. Hope that's okay, captain," Kelly flashed Ember a smile.

"Freaking excuses," Ember replied.

"Just you and me, then," Chris said as he stood. "I really think it's time to go."

"You noticed it closed the door on us, right?" Ember said, her eyes flashing around the room.

"All the more—" Chris didn't see it coming. One second Ember was standing in front of him, the next a giant black shadow swooped silently out of the darkness and slammed into her.

Ember screamed as she was picked up by the biggest spider Chris had ever seen. The thing was swinging from a rope like freaking Tarzan. It let Ember go and she flew through the air to slam into the wall. She bounced off and landed on the pipes. The spider swung up and gripped the far wall, hanging in the darkness like a monstrous Halloween decoration.

Ember stumbled to her feet, her bat still in her hand as she slipped on the pipes under her.

The spider started scampering down the wall, heading straight for Ember.

"Don't even think about it," Chris shouted as he rushed towards it.

The spider froze at the sound, its pink eyes finding him in the darkness. He stepped between the fallen pipes and lunged at the thing. It lifted a claw to swat at him, and Chris flinched, remembering the bruised ribs he'd received last time a spider had back-handed him.

But it missed.

The thing's claw swept through the air inches away him, and he kept moving. Chris' whole weight slamming into the demon. Its legs gave way and it crunched in to the wall behind it. Chris rebounded, landing on his back and summersaulting backwards on the pipes. The spider let out a squeal of pain as it scampered off, slipping over the pipes, and into the darkness at the back on the warehouse.

"Nice one," Ember said. "Freaking Supermanning it. Nice."

"You guys okay?" Kelly shouted. "What's happening?"

"How many are there?" Ivy asked.

"Only one that I can see," Chris said. "But I can't see much . . ."

A light flashed on behind Chris and he spun. Ember held a flashlight in her hand.

"How long have you had that?"

"The whole time. I was trying to sneak up on it."

Ember swept the light over the far wall of the warehouse. Shadows danced and stretched as the light moved. There was a landing up high, covered in thick, demonic cobwebs. It looked like a dozen demon spiders could have made it. The light passed the corner and Chris caught a glimpse of the thing. It was huge, about the size of a Honda Fit, with a reddish pelt. It had a claw raised up over its head, and for a mad second Chris thought it was cowering. More likely it was shading its eight pink eyes from the flashlight.

"How many are you?" Ember shouted.

The thing planted its feet, its hideous, wet mouth moving, its sharp, yellow teeth scraping as it replied in a language Chris couldn't understand.

It charged at them, and Chris bolted at it. With Ivy, Kelly, and Crystal down, they'd be helpless if they let the thing get through. Behind him he could hear Ember clanging over the pipes. Chris reached the demon, his bat raised, and the spider ran right past him.

He stopped, following the demon with his eyes, wondering if it couldn't see him, and he realized it couldn't. It was moving towards Ember and the racket she was making as she struggled to stand.

"Ember, stop," he shouted.

Her left hand held the flashlight, illuminating the monster running towards her, the bat raised in her right arm. The demon stumbled as it reached the debris and Ember charged, letting out a guttural battle cry.

Ember swung just as the spider lifted a claw and slashed. She fell backwards, screaming in pain, and clattering over the pipes once more. The flashlight flew from her hand, sending the shadows spinning wildly for a second before plunging the room into darkness once more.

"No," Chris screamed.

The spider turned at the sound and ran towards him. Chris ducked to his right, pressing up behind the forklift. The spider charged past him, and Chris froze in place, trying to take one breath after another as quietly as possible.

The spider rotated in a slow circle, limping on its foreleg. Something had hurt it, and it was having trouble moving. Its pink eyes passed over Chris without pausing as it turned. The warehouse filled with silence as Ember stopped moving.

The spider let out a shaking breath. "Human," it growled.

The Rhinoceros
and the Fox

FIFTEEN MONTHS AFTER THE WELL

U*gh. Suck butt monkeys,* Ash-Lea thought. *You're looking super cool right now, Ashes.*

She stood in front of the register in the Macey's grocery store, fumbling in her pocket for the crumpled bills that were supposed to be there. She needed one more dollar to pay for the twelve pack of Mountain Dew.

I swear I had enough when I left.

The older lady with the faux-beehive hairdo stood behind the counter, an unimpressed look on her creased face as she waited. Ash-Lea could feel the checkout que growing behind her. Mounting frustration permeated the air between her and the shoppers being trapped in line.

I'm going to need a job. This is embarrassing.

"How much more you need, sweetie?" a white-haired man, two spaces back asked, holding out his credit card to the cashier. "I'll pay for her."

"Wait," Ash-Lea proclaimed, digging into her other pocket. "I got it."

She slapped the extra dollar bill onto the stack on the counter. Beehive took the money, cha-chinged the register, and handed her back the change.

"Thanks, Gramps." Ash-Lea saluted the old man as she scooped up her Mountain Dew and headed for the door.

"The HELL?" another voice shouted from down by the cupcake aisle. "What are you thinking? You're so stupid."

"I'm sorry," another voice, smaller and feminine, replied. "I don't know how it happened. I'm sorry."

Not your business, Ashes, she told herself as her feet stopped walking. *Not your fight.* She lifted her head in the direction of the commotion.

The Macey's wasn't a very big store, all tan linoleum and cream paint from the nineties. It would be impossible for anyone to not hear the guy shouting. He was big; six foot something, with thick arms, a beer-belly, and weird long nose that pointed upwards at the end. He shoved a much smaller woman in the shoulder, hard. She was short, but lithe, with long red hair. She stumbled away, somehow managing to keep her feet.

"The hell you doin? You think we can afford this?" He snatched an item out of the plastic basket hanging on her arm. It looked like a jar of chocolate spread. "You think?"

He took a swipe at her with the jar. She closed her eyes, knowing it was coming, but let the bottle whack her in the cheek.

"I . . . I didn't put it in there," she stammered. "I promise. I didn't."

"Where's the manager?" Ash-Lea asked, looking at the cashier closest to her.

The cashier didn't appear much older than her. He stood with his back to the couple, his body rigid with tension. He looked at Ash-Lea with wide, horror-filled eyes. On his chest was pinned a badge proudly proclaiming MANAGER.

She shoved the case of Dew at him. "Manage this for me, you freaking super hero."

"A—are you making a return?" he stuttered without lifting his arms.

"Oh never mind." Ash-Lea took the case back rather than let the "Manager" drop it.

She started towards the couple. The man with the ugly nose took the woman by the ear and started dragging her towards the nearby emergency exit, cussing at her loudly the whole time. He glanced up at Ash-Lea as she approached, a smile appearing on his face as he pushed on the exit handle.

Ash-Lea figured that would do him in. Across the door in large letters were written the words: 'ALARM WILL SOUND WHEN DOOR IS OPENED.'

He slammed his shoulder into the door and it swung open. An alarm did not sound.

Ash-Lea started running so she wouldn't lose sight of him as he pulled the woman through. She burst out the door and into the alleyway beyond.

The alley was narrow, twenty-foot tall walls blocking out the afternoon sun. Three walls of the alley were cinderblocks, the one in front, behind, and to her left. On her left, a ladder started halfway up the wall, leading to the roof.

To her right where the alley should have opened onto the street, was a pile of four twisted dumpsters, two next to each other and two on top, completely blocking the exit. Ash-Lea's stomach dropped— the dumpsters had been stuffed there deliberately by someone ridiculously strong.

The emergency exit door clicked locked behind Ash-Lea and the two demons, grinning at their brilliant plan, let their disguises melt away.

Ash-Lea felt very stupid as the muscular man turned into a kind of rhinoceros-faced looking dude; his stupid looking nose growing into a long, sharp horn. He was eight-feet-tall wearing a robe of brown cloth draped over one shoulder. He kept his large arms and beer-belly, though those were proportionally huger now, too.

The abused woman straightened and pulled her long hair behind her shoulders. The hair wavered and seemed to grow, flowing over her body like a silken dress—when it was done shimmering over her body, it was the only thing she had on. She fell forward, landing on her hands as they grew into large paws. The same eyes Ash-Lea had seen pleading for help, now looked greedily at her from the face of the biggest fox she had ever seen.

"How did you guys get here?" Ash-Lea asked, keeping her voice level. "I thought the Threshold was busted."

The fox bared her teeth. "I am powerful. Powerful enough to pass across a broken bridge."

"Humble, too," Ash-Lea added. *Does she mean the Threshold? She's strong enough to cross the Threshold without help?*

"Come on," Rhino-Man said, glancing at the fox. "Knock her out."

"I'm trying," the fox said, her black eyes fixed on Ash-Lea's. Her voice sounded weird. Ash-Lea had heard a lot of crazy creatures talk in the last few years, but she'd never heard a fox the size of a pony speak. "She isn't responding."

The fox stared at Ash-Lea for a good ten seconds. Ash-Lea stared back, feeling a little weird, and kinda bored.

"You trying to stare me to death?" Ash-Lea asked. "The trap was really good, but I've got to tell you this is a little anti-climactic."

"Shut up," the fox said.

"What do you mean it's not working?" Rhino-Man asked. "You got her to follow us."

The fox snarled cruelly, piercing Ash-Lea with her black eyes. "She did that on her own, because she's an idiot."

"You kinda got me there," Ash-Lea admitted.

"Maybe she's an Ironsoul," Rhino-Man said.

"Don't be stupid," replied the fox. "Ironsouls are den stories."

"Then why is she still awake?" Rhino-Man asked.

"Oh," Ash-Lea said, catching on to what the demons were talking about. "You're trying to hypnotize me or something so you can kidnap me? That's not happening."

The fox chuffed in frustration. "It's not happening." She clawed at the cement. "Grab her."

Rhino-Man lunged for Ash-Lea, his thick, grey fingers extended. Ash-Lea ducked away, tossing the case of Mountain Dew at the fox's nose. She snapped her jaws and soda exploded everywhere. Rhino-Man barked in surprise, flinching away from the sound as Ash-Lea shot forward, dodging his hand. She kicked off the far wall, jumping up with both arms outstretched, grabbed the cage around the roof-access ladder, and pulled herself up.

"Get her," the fox said, sounding like a freaking movie cliché. *Ugh. So cliché.*

Ash-Lea scampered up the cage and tumbled onto the roof. She spun, drawing the two knives from her belt as she did. She backed away from the alley, her knives held up, praying the demons couldn't follow her onto the roof. But since they could crumple up dumpsters like wads of paper, she wasn't too optimistic.

The roof around her was an acre of flat asphalt tiles, interspaced with air-conditioner units and pipes that stuck out at seemingly random locations. The whole thing was enclosed with a three-foot wall of tan stucco. There wasn't anywhere to go from there but down.

Rhino-Man's heavy foot falls echoed from the alley, his hands suddenly appearing on the roof ledge. His body followed after as Rhino-Man pushed himself into the air to land on the roof, a shockwave rippling through the tiles under her feet. For a second, she hoped he'd be too heavy and would fall straight through. But these things were designed to hold thousands of pounds of snow, and the roof remained intact.

Ash-Lea crouched, her knives held with the blades out. "Looks like it's just you and me, Rocksteady," she said. *I'm going to die,* she thought as she eyed the eight-foot-tall monster looming over her. "What do you want?"

Rhino-Man stalked towards her, his face serious. Ash-Lea stepped to her right, hoping the demon was too focused on her to notice the skylight he was walking straight towards. He was.

His foot hit the dome of plastic and went straight through. Unfortunately, Rhino-Man wasn't as unbalanced as he appeared and paused, looking down at his foot. Rhino-Man withdrew it, the plastic cracking further, and continued towards Ash-Lea, stepping around the skylight.

"I do not harbor ill will against you, human. You're worth gold, and I wish to collect."

"I'm worth gold?" Ash-Lea laughed. *That's a first.* "But there isn't anything special about me."

Rhino-Man laughed dryly. "You're special to the Demonseed. The Winged King knows it."

Holy crapoly. Ash-Lea chuckled in an attempt to cover her shock. *A mother-flipping demi-demon has his sights on me?* "I'm going to have to pass, thanks."

A scrabbling sound from behind Rhino-Man echoed up from the alley. The fox had climbed up the wall, somehow, and was attempting to lift herself onto the roof. She'd gotten her front paws over the ledge, her chin waggling back and forth as she tried to push herself up with her rear legs.

Oh, nah, thought Ash-Lea. *It's already too crowded up here.*

Dancing in a spinning step to her left, Ash-Lea sent a knife whistling through the air under Rhino-Man's arm. It slammed into the fox's throat and she squealed, tumbling backwards into the alley, landing with a loud whump.

"Falron," Rhino-Man exclaimed, taking a step back to glance down the alley. The fox whimpered in response. The demon glared at Ash-Lea, his dark eyes filled with rage. "Now I harbor ill will."

Oh, crap, Ash-Lea held up her one remaining knife. *And I'm down a blade.*

"Falron," Rhino-Man repeated. "Be strong for just a moment while I repay Ash-Lea."

Falron's pained whimper was the only reply.

Rhino-Man focused on Ash-Lea, his hands balling into gigantic, rock-like fists.

"Sounds like she's not doing too good," Ash-Lea said. "Maybe you should just grab her and leave."

He shook his long nose. "Not without you."

"I'm flattered, but I'm already interested in someone."

"I'm interested in gold." He bent over, never taking his eyes from Ash-Lea, and reached for a two-inch-thick pipe sticking out of the roof. His huge hand wrapped around it and he straightened. The pipe tore from the roof effortlessly, a sudden geyser of water spraying Rhino-Man in the leg. He didn't care. Remaining in his hand was four feet of solid iron, the torn ends looking jagged and sharp.

Ash-Lea paced backwards, quickly. "Uh, don't you need me alive?"

"No," Rhino-Man said simply and started across the roof towards her.

Ash-Lea raised her knife defensively but immediately thought the better of it. The roof under her started shaking as Rhino-Man approached, his weapon held over his head. She dove to her right as the pipe shrieked down, cracking into the roof inches behind her heels.

Ash-lea tumbled to her feet and started running. Moments later she felt the roof shaking again as Rhino-Man gained on her. Catching a glimpse of his shadow beside her, she ducked as he jabbed with the pipe, barely missing her back.

Ash-Lea bolted, trying to put as much space between her and the demon, but she felt the roof shaking under her boots no matter how fast she ran.

I can't outrun him, she thought. *Going to have to try fighting him.*

She jumped, planting her feet on an air-conditioner, and sprung back the way she came. Rhino-Man swept the pipe over and she rolled under it, jumping up to her feet. He slammed into the air-conditioner with a boom, stumbling to his knees. The metal groaned and buckled under his weight as he pushed himself up and turned, towering over her. Eight feet seemed like a hell of a lot when it was leering down at you with murder in its eyes.

Ash-Lea sprung off the ground and landed a flying kick into his side. It felt like she was kicking a tree. She bounced off, and stabbed him quickly in the stomach twice. The knife didn't even prick his skin. She danced away, putting ten feet between her and the demon.

Rhino-Man smiled in amusement at her attempts and lunged, whipping the pipe across in a back-handed strike. Ash-Lea stumbled backwards and steadied herself, holding the knife up high.

"You didn't even feel that, did you?"

"I barely noticed it," Rhino-Man said. He wasn't even panting a little bit. "You're brave, but you simply don't have the prowess to fight me. I'll be doing you a favor killing you now."

"How do you figure?"

"I am nothing compared to what you will face if you continue down this path of aiding the Demonseed. Torture you cannot comprehend will be wreaked upon your mind and body. I promise to simply kill you and be done. I need the money. I don't need trouble."

He lifted the pipe high and brought it straight down. Ash-Lea side-stepped the strike and nudged the pipe out of the way with her forearm. Lifting her foot she slammed her boot in his groin.

Rhino-Man gasped, his eyes growing wide, and he fell to one knee. The pipe clattered to the ground as he grabbed his crotch. Ash-Lea snatched up the weapon and spun in a circle, whacking Rhino-

Man across the face. He didn't even flinch. He blinked and focused on Ash-Lea again. Snatching the pipe from her hand with his right, he struck her in the chest with his left fist.

The punch lifted Ash-Lea from the ground and she flew backwards, her breath burning like lava as it was forced from her. She slammed into the roof, rolling over and over, her vision white, her lungs searing as they tried to start working again. Her body eventually stopped tumbling, and she found herself lying on her stomach. She felt the roof under her vibrating and knew he must be close. She glanced up in time to see a huge three-toed foot falling towards her face. She rolled away and clambered to her feet, a hand on her throbbing chest. She had no idea where her knife was.

Rhino-Man stalked forward, apparently no longer in the mood for chitchat, the pipe clutched tightly in his hand.

He's faster than me, stronger than me, and I don't have my knives any more, Ash-Lea thought. *Time for a change of venue.*

Rhino-Man bolted forward, he must have been holding back before, because Ash-Lea barely registered he was running at her before he was swinging the pipe through the air. She dipped and v-lined straight for the skylight. Rhino-Man let out a shout of surprise; he knew what she was trying to do. The roof shook violently as he barreled after her, but despite his speed, she had just enough of a head start to make it.

She reached the skylight and jumped with both feet, praying she had the momentum to not simply bounce off. She felt the tips of his thick fingers brush the back of her head as her feet hit the plastic dome. The plastic shattered around her and she dropped through, the jagged edges ripping at her skin and snagging on her clothes.

She crashed into the top of some shelves and spilled forward, knocking cleaning supplies all over the Macey's aisle. She fell onto her stomach and gripped the shelf under her. *At least I didn't have to go all the way down.*

43

A wave of vertigo swept over her as the shelves lurched sideways, slamming into the shelves next to her and spilling lemon-scented floor polish around her. The racks buckled and crashed onto the floor, Ash-Lea barely keeping a grip on the frame to stop herself from slamming her face. Her arms gave way and she rolled onto her back, lying spread-eagle on the side of the shelving in the middle of Macey's.

Shoppers started gathering around Ash-Lea as she lay on the demolished shelves, taking in deep, lemon-scented breaths. Through the skylight, Rhino-Man glared down at her. The hesitation and resentment on his face was clear. He had no desire to jump down there after her. He was in disguise in the store before, he probably didn't want to get spotted by any humans. *Money, not trouble.*

Then, just faintly, Ash-Lea heard a soft whimpering coming from somewhere outside. Rhino-Man lifted his head, the anger in his eyes being replaced with a deep worry. He dropped the pipe and disappeared.

She hurt, but she'd been beat up before. Considering the rhino was impervious to knives, things could have been much worse. But what really concerned Ash-Lea, was this meant the Threshold could let demonic thugs back through again. That was seriously bad news. Billy and Greyson needed to know immediately.

Ash-Lea clambered to her feet. *Manager* was standing in the aisle, watching her with terror as various cleaners pooled around his sneakers.

She patted him on the shoulder as she limped past. "Clean up on aisle six."

The Wall Between

THREE WEEKS AFTER THE WELL

Billy knew something was wrong the moment he biked into the Blouin's backyard.

The yard itself was huge, with a broad cement pad leading up to the five garage doors. Just beyond the pad, a towering greenhouse contained the swimming pool. The building was obscured by a beautiful dense forest which traced the foot of the mountain.

Visiting the professional demonslayers that lived next door to his best friend was usually a pretty cool experience, with some kind of new demon weapon to study, or a new demon potion to learn about.

But today, a moving truck was parked in the back, its loading ramp pointed towards the garage door which concealed the entrance to the demon-cave. He pedaled down the entrance ramp into the warehouse-sized room. Things inside were worse.

Billy pulled out his flip phone and texted Greyson and Ash-Lea.

Get over to the D.C. Now.

The place was in disarray, especially the medical and tech areas. Lilly—nine feet tall, with bat-like wings and black eyes—was packing, more like dumping, her medical supplies into moving boxes, cursing under her breath as she did.

Celia—eight feet tall, with copper hair and feathery wings—was loading her computer equipment into boxes, though with greater deliberation, a distinct sadness in her countenance.

Osamu the dragon, in his twenty-foot-tall human form, sat by the weapons, his legs crossed, sniffling sadly as he held a handful of spears.

Mr. Blouin, the professional demonslayer (and possibly professional body-builder), stood by the TV, his arms folded as he glared at Seth. Seth loomed over him in his demon form, his muscled arms held tensely by his sides.

"What's going on?" Billy biked across the room and dropped his bike next to the row of military-grade hummers, then ran up to Mr. Blouin and Seth.

They glanced at one another, then Seth spoke. "John has asked us to remove our belongings from his residence," he explained.

Mr. Blouin sucked in a frustrated breath. "Seth refused to allow me a few assurances that would stop a repeat of what happened a few weeks ago. So he cain't stay."

Seth glowered at Mr. Blouin. "I am unwilling to adhere to your petty rules, so you cast us all out."

"I'm protecting my family from you." Mr. Blouin jabbed a finger in the demon's direction.

"There is nothing you could possibly do to protect yourself from me," Seth retorted, his voice stiff. "Any precautions are meaningless, except that they provide *you* with the illusion of safety. I will not participate in a farce."

Mr. Blouin gave a dry laugh. "Call it what you want. But the fact is you won't do it because you're afraid that I might actually be able to kill you if I need to."

"Have you not been listening?" Seth growled. "There is nothing you could do to kill me, human. You are still alive because I will it."

"Oh, threats. You want to keep hanging out at my house, threatening me is not going to help you, man."

"I am not threatening you." Seth leaned towards Mr. Blouin and spoke in a low voice. "I am merely stating a fact."

"Guys," Billy shouted, hoping to redirect their attention before the fists started to fly. "What is going on? Mr. Blouin, why are you kicking the demons out?"

"His trust for us has waxed cold," Lilly called bitterly, tipping her head back as she drunk an amber fluid from a large glass flask. "I offer the utmost medical service in this realm, and he discards me as a paltry spinner of tricks." She slammed the bottle down on the closest table. "'Twill be an arduous chore to descry a seasoned physician worth my *shadow*."

"I ain't dismissing anyone." Mr. Blouin held a hand up to Lilly. "I just think it's time the Brotherhood and the Shield take a step back."

"What the crap?" Greyson said as he appeared behind Billy, riding his bike down the entrance ramp. He lived next door, so it only took him thirty seconds to arrive. "Billy, what's going on?" He dumped his bike on top of Billy's and ran over.

Billy threw up his hands in frustration. "I'm still not sure."

"Greyson," Celia said, her face flush with relief at seeing him. She flapped her huge, feathered wings once to glide across the room and landed in front of him. She gave him a hug. Greyson returned it, giving Billy an odd look. Hugging an eight-foot-tall demon was a bit weird even when she wasn't trembling with frustration.

"I'm sorry, Greyson," Celia said. "We're going to have to find somewhere else to work on the Fidget two-point-ohs."

Greyson took a step back, the news making him speechless for a moment. "Where are you going?"

"I don't know yet. We've got a moving truck outside, but this all just came down this morning. I don't know what I'm going to do."

She turned and looked at her horde of computer equipment. "The Threshold might be stable enough now to let a human drive a truck through to the Demonic Realm, but I couldn't follow. And then the equipment would just deteriorate in a matter of weeks over there. My apartment here isn't big enough."

Greyson put a hand on Celia's arm, she stopped trembling quite so much. "But *why* are you moving?"

Celia gestured hopelessly at Mr. Blouin.

Mr. Blouin walked up to Billy and Greyson, a serious, but tired expression on his face. "It's a precaution," he explained.

"Making enemies out of the toughest people on our team is a precaution?" Billy asked. "Against what? Winning?"

"A sooth declaration, if ever there were," Lilly announced, taking another drink from her flask as she wrapped a cauldron in bubble wrap.

Mr. Blouin grumbled in response. He looked at Billy in a way he probably thought was fatherly, his arms crossed, his head tilted. Considering the circumstances, it was irritating. "Billy, you know what happened when Mr. Fingers took control. It wasn't safe for any of us. I just want to make sure we have as many safeguards in place as possible."

"But this is the demon-cave." Greyson indicated to the room at large. "You can't *not* have demons down here."

Mr. Blouin stared at Greyson, his eyebrows slowly rising. "Since when has my basement been called the demon-cave?"

"That's not what you call it?"

Mr. Blouin blinked. "No, Greyson."

"We can figure this out," Billy said. "There has to be a way we can stay together."

Mr. Blouin let out a rough breath. "I'm not saying the demons cain't still help with your training. I'd just prefer they do it elsewhere."

"Thank you for your permission, John," Seth growled. "We were fine for a hundred years without your assistance. We will be fine once more. The only person this hurts is you."

"I kind of disagree," Greyson said. "I'm just getting the hang of the demon tech Celia's created. Without a place to go . . . I don't know what's going to happen. You can't take that away from me. She's brilliant. We're working on stuff nobody has done before. Even the government doesn't have this tech."

"Mr. Blouin." Celia looked at him with pleading eyes. "Greyson is . . . unbelievably talented. I've never met anyone capable of manipulating demon tech the way he does. We've made more progress in the last year together than I have my whole life."

Greyson shook his hands in excitement. "And this sapphyril metal that Celia has, it's amazing. I can't—"

"Greyson," Mr. Blouin said sharply. "I get it. But I need to protect my family."

"Where is Quinn?" a new voice cut in. Ash-Lea biked down the entrance ramp, taking in the scene with sharp, deep blue eyes. "I don't know what's going on, but smells like more crap than a house full of demonhounds."

Mr. Blouin grunted, the words seeming to come harder the third time he said them. "I'm asking the Shield to remove their belongings from my property."

Ash-Lea biked up to Mr. Blouin and stopped, resting her elbows on the handlebars as she looked up at him. "Since when did you get stupid?"

Mr. Blouin eyes widened. "I'm doing this to protect my family."

"Where is Quinn?" Ash-Lea asked again.

"She's running errands."

"Nah," Ash-Lea replied. "You sent her out because you know she'd tell you this is dumb."

Mr. Blouin pointed at Seth. "That demon," he said, the anger in his voice growing, "struck my Quinn. I aim to see that never happens again."

Ash-Lea didn't respond, likely thinking the same thing as Billy. Quinn was what this boiled down to. Seth had hurt Quinn—knocked her out cold—because she was being controlled by Mr. Fingers. Mr. Blouin didn't like seeing his girl hurt—even if it was to save her life—and especially not by a creature that he was powerless to stop. And perhaps, Ash-Lea was thinking it was best to not point that out to Mr. Blouin right now.

"This isn't a great idea, Mr. Blouin," Ash-Lea said.

"I'm doing what I can to keep my family safe." Mr. Blouin strode over to the stairwell door and yanked it open. "Ya'll have until noon to get out." He disappeared up the stairs, the door closing behind him.

"Well, that sucks monkey butt," Ash-Lea said, watching the stairwell door.

Celia was twisting tape around a monitor, a dismal expression on her face. "I've known Mr. Blouin longer than anyone here. I really thought we were, like, real friends. I get why he's scared, but he's hurting everyone acting like this."

Lilly scooped a dozen small bottles of multicolored medicine into a box. "Alas, a narrow mind rife with pride invariably leads one to judge with emotion and not logic."

A huge snotty, sniffling noise made Billy turn. Osamu had put down the spears, and instead held a handkerchief the size of a baby blanket. He pressed his face into it and blew his nose. It echoed through the room like a truck horn.

"What . . . what did I do wrong?" Osamu asked in a shaking voice.

"Oh, no," Celia flew over to him. She reached up and patted Osamu on the shoulder. "It's not you. Mr. Blouin is just a bit upset right now."

"Concern yourself not over the opinion of those in wrath." Lilly picked up her flask and pointed it at him. "Take no umbrage. 'Tis no slight against your person, but a reflection of the weakness in that man."

"John is doing what he thinks is best," Seth said, seemingly much calmer than he was three minutes before. "He is not simply feeling anger for the harm that has come to his family, but he is feeling fear. He has prepared his whole life to aid the Demonseed, and now the time has come he is experiencing the full weight of that choice; it is expensive, in both means and emotion. Allow him his space. I think in time, he will heal and realize the benefit of working closely with the Shield."

"Perhaps," Lilly said, taking another deep drink from her flask. "But whilst he ruminates, I must relocate the entirety of my stock and implements."

"Plus, he's making Osamu cry," Greyson said. "That just sucks."

"I . . . I'm okay," Osamu said as he buried his face in his handkerchief again.

Billy didn't know what to do. He felt like Osamu needed a hug. But they weren't friends on that level. And the guy was twenty feet tall. The best he could do would be hug his arm, or shin.

"Can we help you pack?" Billy asked.

Osamu sniffled and gave Billy a big smile. "Oh, that's okay. I don't have anything here. Mr. Blouin owns all the weapons."

"Huh," Greyson said. "So you don't have anything to move, and you don't even come over often, but you're still sad about it?"

Osamu nodded, the tears coming back. "I just don't like it when people don't like me."

Billy felt those words deep in his chest. "Mr. Blouin likes you. He's just a bit . . . frustrated right now."

Osamu picked up the spears and began placing them back on the weapons rack. "Maybe."

A crash sounded from the medical area and Lilly cussed in demon. Billy didn't speak demon, but he recognized that word as one the demons used a lot, especially when frustrated. "Curse the flame," Lilly shouted.

The hissing sound, and the black smoke that started to billow up from the floor, was something Billy did not recognize.

Billy ran over to the medical area, where a column of smoke streamed up from the black puddle into the rafters high above his head. "What's happening?"

"Oil of snake gut." She scrunched up her face. "'Tis an effective tonic, but of course combined with cement of Portland, it creates a noxious gas and will transform the cement into a gel. I had not considered the combination until this moment. I never had a purpose to. But since I am expelled, I must consider many things that had not—"

"If it's noxious, shouldn't we be getting away from it?" Billy asked, backing up a step.

"Nay." A wide, slightly manic smile bloomed on Lilly's face. "Let us spread more on the support pillars and watch this human's house fall from under his feet." She let out a cackling laugh.

"Hey," Billy said. "I know you're ticked, but don't burn your bridges yet."

"Burning! A fantastic idea." Lilly picked her flask and took a long drink. "I could concoct a potent accelerant, post haste."

Billy looked at the bottle, then at the feverish glee in her eyes. "Are you drunk?"

Lilly made a dismissive sound. "I am simply lubricating my frustration to enable handling this insult with dignity."

"Seth," Billy called. "Lilly's drunk."

Seth flapped his wings and landed next to them. He put a hand on Lilly's chin and looked into her eyes. "Oh, Lelansiel," he said, kindness in his deep voice.

Lilly pushed him away gently.

The acrid smoke billowing up from the spill on the floor hit Billy and he suddenly felt light headed. "Whoa, I need to get away from this," Billy said, his knees wobbling.

The ceiling space of the demon-cave was quickly filling with black smoke.

"Lilly." Ash-Lea bolted up to the demon and grabbed her by the arm. "What do we need to counteract the oil of snake?"

Lilly looked at the pillar of smoke, her head slanted. "Oil of snake and cement? That gas will kill all of us. We should remove ourselves." She looked up at Seth. "Except you. You are above such things, aren't you? Or beside them. The absence of time allows you to perceive everything. Within eyesight, so to speak. You understand."

Seth's eyes narrowed, and took on a furious, dangerous quality. "Lelansiel, that's quite enough. Tell us how to counteract the oil of snake."

"Gypsum," she said simply.

"Fresh out of gypsum," Ash-Lea said.

"How much?" Seth insisted.

Lilly squinted at the melting cement, and the smoke hissing up from it. "Simply bury it."

"Celia, take care of Lelansiel." Seth considered her with dark eyes. "And see she holds her drunken tongue."

Seth started towards the entrance ramp, then shot out of the cave so fast Billy could barely see him move. *That guy can really jet when he wants to,* Billy thought.

"Come on," Celia said. "Let's take this party outside before we die." She slipped under Lilly's arm and started guiding her towards the ramp.

"Is the computer equipment going to be okay?" Greyson asked, looking ready to grab a box if he needed to.

Lilly let out a guttural laugh. "The boy is more concerned over his toys than his life." She continued laughing.

Greyson gave her an unimpressed look. "That wasn't really an answer," he muttered.

"It's fine, Greyson," Celia said. "We just need to get moving."

"Hey, Osamu," Ash-Lea called. "We got to go."

Osamu nodded sadly and stood. Ash-Lea took his hand, well, she wrapped her hand around his pinky finger, and a small smile broke over his face.

"I'm sorry, Greyson," Celia said as they walked. "We're going to have to work on the Fidgets later. I guess. But I have nowhere to put my stuff."

"HEY!" Greyson shouted so loud Billy jumped. "Bring it over to my place."

"What?" Celia said.

"We have enough room in my garage for that stuff. Just bring it over and we'll put it in there and we'll figure it out later."

"Really?" Celia asked.

"Yea," Greyson said, beaming. "We have a five-car garage. I'll park on the street if we can't fit it in the empty space."

Celia glanced back at her piles of boxes and the huge tangle of wires as they disappeared from view. "I think we could make it fit. But won't your parents mind?"

"Nah," Greyson said. "My mom likes you. And my dad is never around, so he won't care. Let's do it. We even have a work bench out there that we never use. We could keep working on the Fidgets while we figure out a more permanent place."

"Wow, Greyson. That would be great. Thank you." Celia gave a delighted giggle. "I really thought I was going to have to park it in the Demonic Realm. Thank you."

"Ah, no worries. I want to keep working with that sapphyril stuff you showed me. It's super cool."

"It is super cool," Celia agreed. "I think it's what Anarchaist is made out of."

"Really?" Billy asked, the fresh air blowing down the entrance ramp smelled awesome. "What's sapphyril?"

Osamu perked up at that. "It's a metal, but it has the highest affinity to magic than any other material that we know about. That's why it's used in all the most magical weapons."

"Neat-o," Ash-Lea added.

"You'll find the Warrior's Triune are all forged from it, I assume," Osamu said. "It's exceptionally durable. The apprentice Corthas was responsible for several powerful artifacts that are still in existence today, the Triune being the most famous and powerful. He was a master at working magic and sapphyril, possibly greater than the Patriarch himself."

"Oh, right," Billy said. He suspected the topic of the greatest blacksmith was a matter of debate for demonic weapons nerds. The Warrior's Triune were a trio of incredibly powerful weapons, each designed to be the greatest in their realm. Billy happened to have the demonic third of the group in his backpack. He slipped Anarchist out and held it up for Celia and Osamu to inspect.

"That's sapphyril, alright," Osamu said. "The metal in that is worth a thousand times its weight in gold."

Billy looked at Anarchaist, and his mouth started to water. Not only could the weapon shoot lightning out of it when you whack demons over the head, the over-sized, heavy-ass baseball bat he'd been lugging around for the better part of a year was worth a fortune. He could be rich.

"Though I wouldn't recommend selling it," Osamu said. "Its value as an artifact is much greater."

"Yeah," Billy said. *But after I save the world . . .*

"Sapphyril's hard to get a hold of," Celia said. "Especially with the Threshold still damaged. There is a very limited amount of it in the Human Realm."

Osamu nodded. "Much sapphyril in this realm came from the second incursion in the form of weapons the Patriarch forged.

Though there are rumors of a vein of sapphyril being found in Australia."

"Australia?" Celia asked. "That doesn't make sense."

Osamu shrugged.

"Do we have enough of it to keep developing the Fidgets?" Greyson asked.

"Sure," Celia responded. "It's hard to get whether I'm working out of Mr. Blouin's house or not."

"I'll help you get loaded up after the toxic gas clears out," Greyson said.

"Thanks," Celia responded.

"I'm not able to pack boxes yet, but I can carry them," Osamu volunteered.

"Pay me no mind," Lilly piped in, a little too loudly. "I am a capable demon, unneeding of your assistance or kindness."

"I'll help you out," Ash-Lea said. "Let the boys play with their electronics. Maybe you can give me some pointers on your potions while we pack."

"I accept your offer." Lilly slapped Ash-Lea on the shoulder, causing her to stumble. "Males are stricken by a Swargill's copper locks and shimmering wings. Us papabowa are far less favored."

"Tell me about it," Ash-Lea said. "Nobody likes the short girl."

"Nonsense," Lilly replied. "You are exceedingly beautiful."

"And look at you. You're brilliant and tough and nine feet tall. I think you're awesome."

"I appreciate your caring words," Lilly replied. "Though I feel the oil of snake has influenced me more than I realized. I am unsteady on my feet." She patted her robe like she'd forgotten something. "My health tonic remains on the table. I must recover it."

"Everyone knows that's not health tonic." Celia grabbed Lilly's wrist to stop her heading back into the demon-cave.

They reached the top of the ramp, the morning sun was bright and cheerful, the fresh air clearing Billy's head. The moving van, however, darkened his mood immediately.

Celia led Lilly over to a large rock in the garden and helped her sit down. "How about you rest out here and get some fresh air."

A gush of wind passed them and Billy caught a glimpse of Seth flying past, a wheel barrow full of a white powder in his hands.

"What has taken you so long?" Lilly shouted over her shoulder.

A moment later, Seth appeared in the entrance to the demon-cave, not even a bead of sweat on his face from the exertion. "I have smothered the spill."

"Many thanks." Lilly gave Seth a thumbs up, though she didn't seem to have had much practice. "Now open the windows to let the breeze through."

"There aren't any windows down there," Ash-Lea said.

"Once it has cleared out we'll resume loading the boxes," Seth said. "This is barely an inconvenience if you keep focus on the bigger picture. Mr. Blouin may be blind with anger right now, but we are still a team working towards one goal. We should not let his choices distract us."

Billy nodded in agreement, Ash-Lea and Greyson did the same. Moving out of the demon-cave sucked more than Billy could say. But no matter what Mr. Blouin was doing, everyone here was still on the same team. The Demon Gods were still planning to destroy reality. One ticked off dude didn't change anything.

The Failing Princess

SEVEN MONTHS AFTER THE WELL

K rios watched Patricia as she slept. The small human had not been faring well during their time in the Human Realm, and for her to slumber soundly for more than an hour at a time was a gift. She moaned in her sleep and Krios pulled the thin blanket up to her chin. The storehouse in which they hid was insufficiently insulated, the tin walls grew too hot in the earth realm sun, which did nothing to help her fever. They may well have been sheltering under branches by the brackish swamps above the Waterfall Sea, eating welterfly and sharing stories of simpler days. But in the evenings, when the sun hid, the temperature was moderate enough to allow his princess to sleep.

He wasn't sure how much longer they could hide. This place had met their needs for a turn. It allowed him a place to start a fire to cook the food he'd captured. But over the last few days humans had been on the premises, discussing the possibility of purchasing it. Krios did not favor the idea of moving Patricia as she worsened, but he did not know what else to do. Now the season had warmed, they could withdraw into the forests for a time, he supposed.

Patricia rolled over towards Krios and opened her eyes. Too soon she was awake again.

"How do you feel?" Krios asked.

"I am parched," she replied, her voice rough.

Krios retrieved the small, clear container, lifted it to her lips and Patricia drank. The substance humans called plastic was so light, and gave the appearance of fragility, but it was amazingly resilient. Patricia drank deeply through her cracked, trembling lips.

Krios placed his foreleg against her cheek. "You burn like a fire. Did your mother ever tell you about human fevers?"

She shook her head. "We discussed medicines, but most of my education focused on earth languages."

"You were not sick a single day in our realm. This air is toxic to you." He grunted. Invisible foes such as poison offended Krios greatly. Send him an enemy with a sword and he would know what to do, but poisonous air was something one could not defeat in battle. "I do not think it is well for a human to burn for as long as you have."

"Is it possible to find a physician to assist?" Patricia asked weakly.

"We are not near the hospital where I acquired the physician for Prince Melas' birth. But humans are ill frequently. There are hospitals everywhere. I'm sure I can find another."

"I am okay," Patricia said, her words punctuated with a weak cough.

"You are not," Krios said, feeling the words were a repeat of what he had said too recently. In the Demonic Realm she was without peppermint and her human body was disintegrating in the demonic air. Now that her body had been restored, some invisible force in the earth air was infecting her and making her ill in a way Krios did not understand. Demons fell ill, of course, but demon bodies could be treated with glaveroot and other herbs. Each time Krios had entered the Human Realm to slaughter humans, he had never seen anything that even resembled glaveroot.

Patricia didn't respond but let out a long breath as she slept again.

"Sleep, princess." Krios brushed a wayward strand of hair from her face. "I will find the herbs you need."

Krios slid open the door to the storehouse and peered into the bright human night. The moon hung in the electricity-painted sky, glowing like a candle frozen in a sphere. Krios blinked away the cold air which stung his eyes.

He had commonly turned left, heading into the woods beside the storehouses to capture food. But human medicine did not grow in the wilderness, it was fabricated by the magic of human machines and sold in stores. This night, Krios had to turn right.

He shot forward, his claws clicking on the asphalt as he ducked between the tall metal structures. Krios paused as he reached the street, glancing left and right. The lane below was not busy, but the thoroughfare two dozen legs to his right swarmed with human cars, screaming as they flew by. He climbed the wall of the warehouse and slunk forward, crouching low. Squatting behind a low merlon, he peered across the street.

Krios prided himself on his ability to read several human languages, though English was not his strongest. Directly across from him was a shrine for a fallen General by the name of Dollar. Beside it appeared to be a confectioner's store. Next to that was a greengrocer owned by an individual whose name was Smith.

"Food and drugs," Krios read. *Drugs*, he realized. *That's the human name for medicinal herbs.*

The night was not late, and dozens of humans continued in and out of the greengrocer. It would be impossible to enter the building unseen. And once inside, how was he to tell which drugs would be of benefit to Patricia?

I must enlist the aid of a human, Krios decided.

Looking about, there were not many options to cross the road without attracting the attention of the nearby civilians. Krios was considering finding a way around when he noticed a huge tower looming over the warehouse. It was formed of intersecting bars of metal, it stood at least sixty legs high. Several thick metal cables extended from the structure and connected to another past Smith's store. Beyond that the cables continued, joining tower to tower until they disappeared in the darkness. It was high enough in the dark night that it was unlikely a human would spot him.

Krios ran across the roof and leapt into the air, gripping the metal bars and slowing his momentum silently. He scurried up the edifice until he reached the top, and paused. The view of the surrounding area was a sight to behold. The humans had created roads and vehicles that swirled about in all directions. Lights glistened from storefronts and lamps that stretched for leagues. There were hundreds of thousands of humans just within his eyesight.

The demon gods wish to fight them? With their electronics and firearms, it seems a foolish notion.

The humans were not all soldiers, but they would defend their land, as any civilian would when presented with an invading host. The time was fast approaching that they would all face that choice.

But I must bind one fly at a time. Patricia is in need of medicine.

Krios climbed to the apex of the tower and placed a claw on the cable which connected to the next tower. A peculiar, tingling sensation rushed through his body, every hair on his thorax stood on end.

How odd, Krios thought. He couldn't fathom what magic surged through the metal rope that would make his whole frame prickle. There was something about the human magic that he didn't like. Hanging from the cable, he rushed across as fast as he could, his eight claws gripping the narrow rope.

The wire stretched over the road, the parking lot, and Smith's store. When he was above the roof of the store, Krios produced a length of spider rope and whipped it around the cable. He dropped from the wire, glad to be free of it and the buzzing magic, and plummeted through the artificial-orange air. The rope stopped his descent a leg from the roof of the store, and he dropped soundlessly onto it.

A curious, burning smell wafted through the air. Krios crept across the roof and peered over the rearmost wall of the store. The back lot of the store was not brightly lit, a large square of asphalt with several cars parked in the shadows. Around the asphalt unkempt shrubs grew, entangling themselves about a sagging metal fence. To Krios' left, a ramp descended towards a huge door in the rear of Smith's store.

Directly beneath him, a single human stood in the dim light. She did not seem large by human standards, with a slim figure and thin arms. Her outfit of black pants and a red collared shirt held the air a uniform. She tucked her short brown hair behind her ear and lifted a small stick to her lips. When she lowered the stick, a cloud which wreaked of burning lifted into the air, much like a demon smoking a pipe, though far less fragrant.

"Human," Krios grunted in human language.

The woman started in surprise, looking around her for the source of the voice.

"I require drugs," Krios said. "Are you able to help me?"

The human laughed nervously. "How do I know you're not a cop?"

"I can assure you, I am not." *Whatever that is.* "Can you help me locate drugs?"

"Yeah. I might," she said. "What are you looking for?"

Krios dropped from the roof and landed in front of the human. "Excellent. I require your assistance immediately."

The woman screamed and jumped backwards, tumbling over the rail behind her and down the ramp. The burning stick flew into the air, drawing an arc of bitter smoke as it fell.

Krios dashed forward after her, following her down the incline. She scuttled backwards on her hands, her eyes bulging as she took in Krios' mighty form, until she slammed into the far wall. Her mouth was wide, her body shaking. The only thing she seemed to remember to do was breathe.

"Will you assist me?" Krios asked.

Her eyes passed over Krios, and landed on his sapphyril mandible. "Why can you . . . talk?" she said. "Please don't eat me."

"I will not eat you," Krios said as reassuringly as possible.

She continued her attempts to scuttle backwards, despite the wall hindering any further movement. "What . . . what . . . what do you want?"

Krios rolled his eyes. Humans become quite stupid when you frighten them. "I told you, I require drugs."

She laughed, though without humor. "I ain't got a bowl big enough for you."

Patricia did not have time for this human to continue blubbering nonsense. "Cease panicking. I require assistance."

"Then you'll bite my head off?" she asked.

Krios grumbled. Startling humans was perhaps counterproductive when one needed aid. "I promise that I will not harm you if you provide the assistance I require."

The human nodded. "Yeah, okay. Sure."

"What is your name?" Krios asked.

"My name?" She stared at Krios as if she did not understand the question. "Heh. Me . . . Melissa."

"Melissa. That is a lovely name," Krios said with a smile.

Melissa gripped her head with both hands. "Holy crap, what is happening?"

"Melissa, my name is Krios. Can you assist me with acquiring drugs?"

"What kind of drugs does a thing like you need?"

"I need anything that will cure a human fever."

"A . . . a what? A human fever? Oh," she gave a small laugh. "You mean you want medicine? Like for a person?"

"Yes." Krios did not understand how he had not been clear.

"Why do you need something like that?"

Krios did not feel like explaining himself to a nobody, but putting someone at ease when one required assistance was important. "My . . . friend is ill. She is a human and I do not understand human medicine enough to assist her. I do not belong in this place."

"No freaking joke."

"Please, Melissa," Krios said, his voice softer than intended. "I fear for my friend's life."

Melissa pulled another stick from pocket on her shirt, her hands trembling. She placed the stick between her lips. Casting some kind of human spell, a flame appeared on her hands, igniting it. She inhaled through the burning stick again and let out a cloud of smoke. "What's wrong with her? What symptoms does she have?"

"She burns with fever. She has experienced mucus discharge from her nose, and her bowel movements have been inconsistent."

"Okay." Melissa started to stand, but her arms gave way. "You promise to let me go if I help?'

"I have no intention of harming you. My princess is in grave need of assistance. She is my primary concern."

Melissa's face contorted with confusion. "Your princess?"

"Yes."

"Your princess is a human, and she's sick, and you're here getting drugs for her." Melissa spoke as if she was simply repeating previously stated facts to herself for no purpose other than to waste time.

Krios felt frustration rising inside him, but he kept it out of his voice. "Yes, that is the case."

Melissa looked at her shoes and shook her head. "Do you have money?"

"No."

She groaned, then sucked on the burning stick. "I'll lose my job if I go in there and steal it for you."

"Patricia may lose her life if you do not. I will be willing to steal it if you tell me what she needs."

"That's probably not the best idea. You are the scariest thing that I have ever seen. But heaven help me, you have honest eyes." Melissa stood up and walked sideways in shifting steps around Krios. "I freaking whacked my head falling down here. I need some ibuprofen anyway. Just give me a few minutes."

Krios watched Melissa walk up the ramp and around the railing. She dropped the burning stick, stomping it out on the ground, before disappearing through the door. He climbed up the wall and settled down onto the roof. The minutes slipped past and Melissa did not emerge. He wasn't sure how Smith pedaled his medicines, but he had better not take too long or Krios would have to go in there and take them by force. But as long as Smith did not have a gun, that wouldn't be a problem.

After fifteen human minutes, the door below Krios opened and Melissa emerged. In her arms were half a dozen white sacks full of small bottles.

"Hey," Melissa said. "Krios, you here? You better be, this wasn't cheap."

Krios stood. "I am."

Melissa jumped in surprise and looked up at him. "You have to stop sneaking up on me. For a minute I'd hoped I was tripping and you weren't really here at all."

"You wish to trip again?" Krios asked. "Do you enjoy hitting your head?"

"No." She held up the bags. "Just come here so I can explain this crap."

Krios leaned over the side of the building, studying the sacks in Melissa's hands. "So many," he said. "How many do I give her?"

"Someone your size? I don't know."

"She isn't my size. She's a human. No more than ten years old."

"What?" Melissa blinked. "I figured she was as big as you, for some reason. She's a little kid? What are you doing with a little kid?"

"She is my princess. I am protecting her."

"Okay." Melissa shook her head in dismay as she pulled a bottle out of the bag. "Can you read? I'm guessing so, you can talk. The dosage is on the bottle. If she's ten then you give her one of these for the fever every four hours. For the diarrhea—"

"The what?"

"For the *inconsistent bowel movements*, give her one of these every four hours until things stop up. Give her lots of water. Do you have water?"

"We do."

"What food do you have for her?"

"I have been hunting. Some birds, small rodents."

That statement seemed to surprise the human more than when he jumped off the roof in front of her. She stood speechless for a moment. "You what? She's human, right?"

"She is."

"Freaking hell. Hold this." She held out the bags. Krios looked at them, unsure what she wished for him to do. "Hold out your arm-leg-thingie." Krios extended his foreleg and she slipped the sacks over his leg. "I'll be back." She strode back into the store and was gone.

Krios stood there, not sure what he was supposed to do now. He had the medicines, but he did not know how to use them. He didn't have time to waste indulging Melissa's impulsiveness.

Just as Krios had decided it was time to leave, Melissa emerged from the store with more bags. "I got you some human food. Granola bars, juice, crackers. Some nuts. Some apples."

"Ah, thank you," Krios replied. "I'm sure Patricia will enjoy these." They weren't roast welterfly, but birds simply did not have much meat on them.

Melissa's face twisted, giving Krios a look ripe with disgust. "Just stop feeding her rats, man. Okay?"

"As you say," Krios agreed.

"Just . . . you know where to find me when you run out, okay? I'm out here most nights. Just wait until I come out to smoke. If I'm not here one night, I'll be here the next. And this cost me everything I had left, so if you could pay me back somehow, I'd appreciate it."

"I will endeavor to do so."

Melissa looked Krios up and down, shuddering at the sight of his fearsome countenance. "You're a good guy, right?"

"It is my sole duty to take care of my princess. That is all."

Melissa drew another stick from her pocket and set it alight, her fingers shaking. "I . . . I don't know how to process what is happening tonight. I am probably not going to believe it happened when I wake up tomorrow."

"I should not allow you to live. If word of my location spreads, my princess will be in danger." Krios lifted his foreleg, his claw extended towards the human's throat.

Melissa lurched backwards, stumbling into the wall behind her. "You promised you wouldn't hurt me," she whimpered.

"That I did." Krios gripped the wall behind Melissa's head and climbed onto the roof. He turned back, looking down on the little human. She sat on the ground, her face pale as she gazed at his mighty form looming above her in the orange night. "You have saved a life today, Melissa. You have my gratitude, and the gratitude of the Spider Horde."

Krios rushed back to Patricia, the odd white sacks over his arms, his hope for her life entirely in the human medicines.

A Big Help

EIGHT MONTHS AFTER THE WELL

Osamu lay beside a bubbling stream, enjoying the sun as it warmed his scales. He stretched out his claws and yawned, smoke drifting from his dragon nostrils painting the air. He rolled onto his back and looked up at the towering trees above him. Osamu loved being in the forest where he was surrounded by things bigger than himself; almost as amazing as being in a human city. Though he could never feel totally at ease there. He couldn't twirl around the buildings as he wished. Someday, though, he dreamed of soaring in and out of skyscrapers; once peace was established with the humans and he was free to do something so ridiculously fun.

But for now, life was good. He hadn't had to fight in months. Word had spread about the Demonblood's defeat of Mr. Fingers, and it seemed demons simply weren't interested in hurting Billy anymore. Rumor was that the Winged King kept a constant vigil over Mr. Fingers as he recovered, so he was no longer attempting to attack Billy either.

Though, that news concerned Osamu. The Winged King was responsible for maintaining peace across his domain, which included the dragon kingdom beyond the Glass Sea. If the tension between the elephants and dragons escalated, there would be so much bloodshed. The Lord Dragon was patient but met offense with great retribution. *I hope my sisters are doing okay,* he thought. His nephews would still be small, but learning to speak. He wouldn't be there for their first breathing, either. Osamu chuckled to himself. He'd set his grandmother's rug aflame during his first breathing. His mother, roaring in surprise, had thrown it into the river to stop the house from burning down. To this day he wasn't sure his father knew what really happened to his beloved rug.

Osamu straightened his front legs, and sat on his rump, the sense of peace fading. He'd been gone from his family for many years now. They didn't understand why he needed to protect the Demonseed, but they did not stop him either. His big sister, Laisuma, had laid her first clutch of eggs only weeks before he left. *I miss her, and her warmth.*

Osamu stood and stretched, shaking the dust from his scales. He had the rest of the day off but he no longer felt like relaxing. Perhaps he'd go to the library and read some more on Apache Helicopters. He bowed his head over the stream and began to drink. The water cooled his dry throat, reminding him that, at least for now, things were peaceful.

A loud popping sound echoed in his ears as the light and space in front of him puckered—the telltale sign of a demonic gate. A spider with a small white wyvern perched on his head slipped through and landed on the opposite side of the stream.

Osamu spat the water out in surprise, drenching the newcomers.

The tremanchen, though the smallest tremanchen Osamu had ever seen, sputtered and wiped his eyes with the back of his claw. The wyvern shook her scales dry.

"Are you Osamu?" the spider asked, otherwise ignoring the water dripping from his hair.

Osamu, too surprised to speak, nodded.

"My name is Aesop," he said.

"Oh!" Osamu exclaimed, sitting down and laying his head on the ground so he came as close as possible to look the spider in the eye. "You're the spider who lives with Selanthiel."

"It's nice to finally meet you," Aesop said, shaking water from his forelegs.

"How did you find me?" Osamu asked.

"Belphegan did." Aesop pointed to the wyvern on his head.

"A messenger," Osamu said to the tiny white wyvern. Wyverns and dragons were not the same race, but they held the utmost respect for one another. "A pleasure."

Belphegan nodded in greeting.

Osamu looked back at Aesop. "Quite a talented messenger to bring you through her gateway."

"She is," Aesop agreed. "Strongest messenger wyvern I've ever seen. Though I haven't seen many."

"What can I do for you?" Osamu asked.

"Everyone is gone and . . . and I'm in over my head. I need you to come to Ash-Lea's house. Do you know where that is?"

"I do. What's happen—"

"Wonderful." Aesop did a little jump and clicked his claws together joyously.

"Ash-Lea lives quite a ways away from here." Osamu gave an apologetic frown and sat up. "I was hoping to take care of some personal matters first."

"I don't really have time," Aesop replied, a nervous laugh on his mandibles.

"I supposed I—"

"Thank you," Aesop said, grinning from eye to eye. "Let's go."

Belphegan flapped her wings and swooped over onto Osamu's head. Her tiny claws gripped the scales between his eyes and he felt a gargantuan tug. The world turned black as space folded around him, and Osamu's stomach dropped like the ground had suddenly disappeared.

Osamu yelped, his legs flailing as he realized the ground *had* disappeared from under him. He was in the air, several dozen wings above Ash-Lea's house. It took a second of gut-churning freefall for him to adjust and start flying under his own power. Sliding through the air towards Ash-Lea's back yard, he turned in a wide circle to give himself enough time to slow. He shrunk into his human form as he touched down. Although he had been practicing his human form, it wasn't very good yet. He still stood about eighteen feet high, easily able to see over the roof of the house.

Osamu understood immediately why Aesop sounded so concerned. Someone had let the demonhounds loose in Ash-Lea's back yard without any restraints or consideration for Ash-Lea's property.

Flame Monster, his black ears flopping merrily, chased the brown puppy, Zarcon, in a circle around a tall, dead tree in the back yard, shooting out small puffs of fire as he did. Osamu couldn't tell if Zarcon thought this was fun or not, she snapped over her shoulder as she ran. The biggest concern was the dozen or so small fires Flame Monster had started in the dry grass. The pale Charles Barksley was standing against the side of the garage, scratching through the wall while siding flew all around him. Oodles was by the back fence, her red fur stained brown as she dug *another* giant hole, barking joyously as she worked.

"Oh, no," Osamu said. "Belphegan, please get Aesop. I need help."

Belphegan chuffed out a breath and walked over to the overgrown garden. She turned in a circle under the stone bench and lay down, putting her head under her wing.

"I need help," Osamu called to the wyvern. "Please."

Belphegan gave a chittering snore in response. Messengers were usually only able to open gateways for themselves and a piece of parchment. The really special ones could carry gifts to other kingdoms. He'd never heard of a messenger that could transport another demon, especially a Fildoran a thousand times her size. The effort must have exhausted her entirely, which meant Osamu was on his own for now.

Flame Monster let loose a jet of fire in Zarcon's direction and a swath of dry grass under the tree burst into flame. Zarcon whimpered as the fire brushed her back and she started sprinting in tight circles. Osamu rushed over, stomping out the small blaze with his foot.

"Bad demonhound." Osamu frowned at Flame Monster.

Flame Monster rounded on Osamu and began snapping playfully at his heels.

Osamu started dancing on his toes, sending vibrations through the ground that shook the house windows. "No, Flame Monster. Stop that."

With a crunch, Charles Barksley tore off a section of the siding on the garage and began shaking it violently, warbling snarls rising from his throat.

"Mother's smoke!" Osamu shouted in surprise and ran over. He tugged the siding out of the hound's mouth, but Charles didn't let it go. He hung on to it, shaking as he tried to yank the wood from Osamu's hand.

Sharp agony shot up Osamu's leg as Flame Monster clamped down onto his ankle. He let out a hoot of pain and started dancing in a circle on one foot, the demonhound hanging from the other.

Oodles was content to continue digging. She was on her fifth hole, her stumpy tail barely visible above the rim.

Zarcon looked relieved that something else had taken Flame Monster's attention and trotted over to Belphegan to investigate the newcomer.

A hound still on his ankle and another one dangling from the siding in his hand, Osamu called, "Zarcon, don't get too close. I'm not sure she's going to—"

Belphegan woke up and snapped at Zarcon's nose. She yipped in pain and shot off towards one of Oodles' holes. She jumped in and turned around, poking her head above the edge, her little ears shaking.

Flame Monster released Osamu's ankle long enough to lick his lips and lunge in for another attack. He could barely open his mouth wide enough to fit a part of Osamu's ankle in his jaws, but his teeth were sharp enough to pierce his skin. Osamu howled in pain again.

Charles had decided he'd had enough of dangling from the siding, and dropped. He dashed over to the garage, yipping happily as he started tearing off another piece.

"Charles Barksley, you stop that," Osamu shouted as Flame Monster lunged in for another attack.

That was the end of Osamu's patience.

He dropped his human form, erupting into a dragon far too big for the back yard, his tail end spilling over the fence and down the driveway. He stretched his head forward, brushing against the dead tree. The tree let out a crack from the ground to the top branches.

"STOP . . . IT," Osamu roared, shaking windows up and down the street, a car alarm sounding from somewhere far away.

Oodles poked her head out of the hole she'd been digging, curiosity in her big eyes at the humongous dragon glaring at her. Flame Monster had flown off Osamu's toe when it turned into a giant dragon claw. He rolled onto his feet and trotted over to sit next to Oodles. Charles Barksley dropped his mouthful of siding and sat on his haunches, looking up at the dragon towering above him and cocking his head. Zarcon ducked down further into the hole, trembling so much she could barely stand.

"That's enough of that, houndlings," Osamu the dragon growled.

Flame Monster stood up and started off like he had better things to do. Osamu puffed out a black cloud of smoke that filled the back yard. Flame Monster sneezed and sat back down.

"Now," Osamu said. "Can any of you tell me where everyone is?"

Charles Barksley scratched behind his ear.

Osamu tapped the ground impatiently with his whiskers. "Of course you can't. We're just going to sit here being good houndlings until Aesop returns and explains what is going on."

Osamu glanced over to the garden. Belphegan was asleep again. Turning back to the hounds, Flame Monster had moved slightly towards the hole where Zarcon was hiding.

"I don't think so, Flame Monster," Osamu said. "Charles," Osamu turned to the white demonhound. "What are you doing here? Aren't you usually with Quinn?"

Charles Barksley let out a low whine at the mention of his human.

"I was enjoying a day warming myself in the sun in the mountains. Now, for reasons unknown, I'm here keeping an eye on you four so you do not destroy Ash-Lea's house. What did she do to deserve this? Oodles? Digging holes. You are being a very naughty houndling."

Oodles pressed her ears back against her head and whimpered pitifully.

"No, you will not evoke sympathy now." Osamu looked directly at Flame Monster. "My ankle still hurts from your games." The demonhound stared right back at him, innocence painted on his demonic face.

"Belphegan," Osamu called. "I'd like it if you'd wake up now. Some human will think a cloud resting in Ash-Lea's driveway is somewhat out of place."

Belphegan snored again.

Osamu glanced over his shoulder. The wyvern showed no signs of waking up. When he looked back, Flame Monster was sitting by the garage.

"I'll have none of that," Osamu said. He extended his whisker and picked up Flame Monster with it. He'd always thought his whiskers were small things, but compared to the demonhound puppies they were huge, able to wrap all around their bodies. The little demonhound's legs flailed as he was moved through the air. Osamu plopped the animal in one of the holes Oodles' had dug. "You, too," he said to Charles, nudging him into another hole with his whisker.

The four demonhounds stared up at Osamu. Flame Monster twisted his head to the side and sneezed, letting out a small jet of fire in Zarcon's direction. Zarcon ducked into her hole, whimpering. Osamu directed a warning growl at the stubborn demonhound.

"Flame Monster," Osamu said sternly. He billowed out a huge plume of smoke directly onto Flame Monster's muzzle. When the smoke cleared, Zarcon was covered from ear to paw in ash. He sneezed, and shook his head, a cloud of grey dust rising from his fur.

"My fire is bigger than yours, houndling. Do not test me." Osamu looked down at the four puppies staring up at him. "Now, what to do with you until Belphegan awakes? I don't suppose you'd be interested in hearing about F-16 fighter jets? They are fascinating machines."

Barksley seemed to have already grown bored with the lecture. He climbed out of the hole and started back towards the garage. Osamu lifted his whisker and scooted the puppy back into place.

"Well, what do you want to do? Besides destroying Ash-Lea's house and burning up her yard?"

Flame Monster shook his head again.

"Don't get smart with me," Osamu told him.

Oodles gave a wide yawn, turned in a circle and lay her head on her paws. Osamu couldn't resist the urge, and gave a window-rattling yawn himself. "Not a bad idea, Oodles. Perhaps we could all use a nap."

In response, Flame Monster started bouncing up and down, Zarcon cowered further into her hole, and Barksley bolted for the garage to begin attacking the wall again.

"No, no, no," Osamu said. He turned to grab Barksley with his whisker and Zarcon immediately started whimpering. Osamu looked back to see Flame Monster standing at the edge of the hole Zarcon hid in, barking at her.

"Stop being a bully," Osamu said. Flame Monster didn't stop. "What do you need to calm down?"

Then a thought occurred to Osamu. *What do I need when I'm frustrated?*

Osamu melted into his human form and picked Flame Monster up by the scruff of his neck. Flame Monster bucked and snipped at Osamu's fingers defiantly. Osamu sat cross-legged on the ground, placed the demonhound in his lap and started scratching behind his ears. Flame Monster stopped fighting, but he continued growling.

Barksley cocked his head at Osamu as if to ask why Flame Monster was getting all the attention. He trotted over and nudged Osamu's other hand. Osamu put that puppy in his lap and started scratching him, too. It only took Oodles a minute to notice what was happening. She sleepily crawled out of the hole, trudged over to Osamu's lap, squeezed in between her brothers, and fell back to sleep.

Osamu smiled at Zarcon. "Come here, girl. It's okay."

Zarcon whimpered, but slowly climbed out of the hole, her head down. She climbed up onto Osamu's lap reluctantly, staying as far away from Flame Monster as possible. Flame Monster saw her and jumped over to give her a friendly lick on the face, then positioned himself under Osamu's hand again.

"Okay. Are we all good?" Osamu asked.

Flame Monster pushed his head into Osamu's fingers, instructing him to resume scratching. The other puppies seemed to be falling asleep.

"Good. You houndlings keep behaving. Ash-Lea's parents do not deserve to have their home destroyed by your antics." Osamu yawned again. He scooted backwards and leaned against the tree. "This was not what I had planned for my day off, but you certainly are cute little things."

The sun emerged from behind a cloud, warming Osamu's face and he closed his eyes. For a moment, life felt peaceful once more.

Osamu awoke as he felt someone shaking his arm. He sat bolt upright, fearing he'd failed his duty, but was relieved to see four sleeping puppies still in his lap. Beside him stood a tired-looking Aesop, worry in his eight eyes.

"Oh, my. Are you okay?" Aesop said. "What happened? When I realized Belphegan wasn't coming back I started running."

Osamu stretched his arms. "We were leagues out of the city. It would have taken you all day just to reach the nearest house."

"Oh," Aesop said, panting. "I didn't know that." He let out a long breath. "Looks like you have everything under control." He scratched the back of Zarcon's head.

Osamu glared down at the little tremanchen. "Yes, I suppose I do. Where is everyone? These hounds almost destroyed Ash-Lea's home." He picked up the broken piece of siding and showed it to Aesop.

"Seth set up this training activity for Billy that they all went to," Aesop explained.

That was interesting news indeed. "Is Mr. Blouin okay with the Shield now? I haven't talked to him since he kicked us out of his house."

"I've never talked to him myself. But from what Selanthiel says, I think he's coming around. They're all together today. But they didn't have anyone to watch the demonhounds, so they asked me to do it last minute."

"They could have asked me," Osamu stated.

"They didn't want to bother you on your day off."

"Don't you have days off?"

Aesop shrugged. "I don't really have any days on, so I don't have any days off, either."

Charles Barksley woke up and climbed down from Osamu's lap. He casually walked over to the discarded piece of siding, picked it up and started dragging it away.

"Don't even think about it," Osamu ordered.

Barksley dropped the siding, cocked his head at Osamu, then trotted back over and sat in his lap.

Osamu patted Charles Barksley thoughtfully. "I'll have a talk to Selanthiel about springing chores on you without warning, or proper preparation. It was unfair to place you in this position."

Aesop gave a wan smile. "I was just happy to help. I'm sorry I messed up."

"You didn't mess up at all. You got help when you needed. Most spiders I've met would have let Ash-Lea's house burn down before they dared seek assistance. It can take a big spider to ask for help."

Aesop beamed up at Osamu. "Nobody's ever called me a big spider before."

"It's the spider inside that counts." Osamu patted Aesop on the head.

Aesop, seemingly overcome, darted in a quick circle. "Thank you, Osamu. And thanks for helping out a stranger."

"There are no strangers in the Shield, only demons we haven't met yet." Osamu considered the four sleeping puppies in his lap. "Are Quinn, Billy, Ash-Lea, and Greyson ready to take care of their hounds yet?"

"Not yet. They'll be back tomorrow."

"Tomorrow?" Osamu exclaimed.

Flame Monster sat up at the sound, little puffs of smoke drifting from his nostrils as he grinned up at Osamu.

Super Sucky Pøwers

SIX MONTHS AFTER THE WELL.

It was exactly fourteen months to the day until Billy could walk
out of the foster system and his foster parent's house for good.

But who's counting? Billy thought.

"Are you listening?" Belinda, Billy's foster mom, asked.

"Yes." Billy nodded.

"What did I just say?"

"Oh, listening to you? No. Sorry."

"You are such a smart aleck sometimes, Billy. Look at this." She
pointed at the open cupboard, in which the cups were stacked. "Do
you see what's wrong with this?"

"I . . . I don't." He honestly couldn't. They were cups in a
cupboard. What else did she want?

"They're a mess. They need to be stacked in order. Big ones on
the left, small ones in the middle, coffee mugs on the right with their
handle towards the wall. If they're just shoved in there, you're going
to knock something to the floor when you go in to get them."

Billy had hoped to get some reading in. A Saturday with nothing planned was pretty rare these days. Usually on a Saturday he had a half day loading pallets at the salt factory, then some kind of demon practice with Seth or Mr. Blouin, but he had nothing on his schedule today. For the first time in ages, he was free. Billy had an ominous feeling he was about to spend the day reorganizing the cup cupboard.

"Fix this," Belinda ordered. "Please," she added. "I don't want anything to break."

Billy knew better than to fight with Belinda over stupid stuff. Especially when it was as simple as reorganizing the cups. It would take him ten minutes at most and then he could hide at the park and read. He started pulling the cups out of the cupboard and organizing them on the counter. Belinda nodded maternally, then swept from the room.

But it wasn't that simple. Just doing what he was told—or not doing it—wasn't straightforward anymore. Over the winter, Billy had had a weird experience. A colony of people had been living inside his blood for a few years now—in the reality contained in the matrix formed by his blood, to be specific. And over the winter, one of those people had showed him a trick, *a technique?* She taught him how to read the thoughts and emotions of people—to understand them better. He wasn't reading minds like a psychic, but he had a sense of people's intentions and motivations. Problem was, she hadn't shown him how to control it. So now it kind of just popped on and off without his permission.

The result of the emotion-reading-super-power was when Belinda told him off for messing up the cup cupboard, he *kind of* got where she was coming from. Sure she liked being neat and hygienic, but there was an underlying need for cleanliness that drove her. Billy wasn't even positive she knew it was there. But it felt like a steady drum beat keeping time in her life. Neat cups were important to her. So without even thinking about it before that moment, it was suddenly important to Billy, too. The whole thing sorta sucked. Understanding people made it really hard to be stubborn when he felt like it.

Just as Billy was replacing the cups, Belinda walked into the backyard wearing some old coveralls and a wide sunhat. He glanced up and saw Steve already out there, shovel in hand. He didn't know what they had planned for the garden, but if they were back there he might even be able to sit in the formal dining room to read instead of disappearing somewhere not air-conditioned.

Billy carefully slid the last coffee mug back in place and closed the cupboard door when the shouting started from outside.

Don't get involved, Billy told himself. *None of your business.*

But something about the note of hopelessness in Belinda's voice made him stop and listen. The emotion-reading had subsided as he worked, but he still knew what frustration sounded like. He walked to the back door and peeked through the window. Steve stood beside the old tree stump that had been in the back yard for years, a shovel in his hand. Belinda stood across from him, her arms folded. Beside them was a stack of mulch in large plastic sacks, and some plastic garden borders; fancy ones, not the cheap kind. It looked like the Fosters were finally putting in the garden they had been talking about for years.

Steve kicked the stump. "I need to get the Tahoe back here, so I can pull it out."

"Just rent a grinder from Home Depot," Belinda said.

"You know how much mess a grinder makes?" Steve thrust the shovel into the grass. "I'm not paying a hundred bucks to make a bigger mess back here."

Belinda threw up her hands. "You'll knock down the fence if you try to get the car back here."

Steve pointed to the gate, then the stump, then the gate again. "It's the only way."

81

Billy opened the back door. *What are you doing?* He slipped into his boots and walked up to the couple. *Don't get involved, idiot.* "Hey, anything I can do to help?"

Steve and Belinda stared at Billy for at least ten seconds, trying to process what he had said.

"Uh, yeah," Steve said. "Trying to pull the stump out, so we can plant the garden. I'm thinking we can get the Tahoe back here to pull it out."

Billy looked up at the gate. It was pretty wide, but not wider than Steve's car, especially because he'd have to angle it in from the driveway, which was not very broad. "I don't think we'll get the Tahoe back here. How long is the chain? Can we leave the car in the driveway?"

Steve's eyes grew wide with excitement, and Belinda gave a little jump.

"Billy, great job," Steve patted Billy on the shoulder as he headed into the garage.

Steve emerged a minute later with a huge length of chain. He strung it around the stump, slipping it through holes under the roots he'd been digging, then pulled the other end of the chain towards the driveway.

"Ah, crap," Steve said, tugging on the chain as he stood on the other side of the gate. "Look, the angle is off. If I put it on the Tahoe and pull it tight, it's going to rub against the gate there. That'll pull it down for sure."

"Just get the grinder," Belinda said.

"I am not getting a grinder," Steve shot back, pulling on the chain. It banged against the gate. "I can figure this out."

Steve climbed into the Tahoe and drove half way down the driveway. He stopped and reversed, angling the tow bar towards the opening. He slowed, the brake lights flashing as he pumped the brakes, the car growing closer and closer to the fence.

"He's not going to fit," Billy said to Belinda.

"Steve," Belinda shouted. "Steve, stop. You're going to knock over the fence. Steve! Get out of the damn car."

Steve climbed out of the car and slammed the door. He swore loudly and kicked the gate. "I could probably pull up this section of fence."

Belinda pulled off her hat and slapped it against her thigh. "That would be just as much mess as renting a grinder."

"Rent a grinder, rent a grinder," he said mockingly. "Do you have any other ideas?"

"No, because it's a damn good idea, and you're being an ass."

Billy hated seeing them fight. He picked up the chain and pulled it tight, trying to see if there was an angle that it could go through the gate to the driveway without damaging the gate. There just wasn't a way to make it work. Renting the grinder was probably the best option, but he didn't feel like telling Steve that.

Billy tugged on the chain again and felt the stump lift half an inch. He tugged again, the stump groaning in protest. Gripping the chain with both hands he leaned backwards, pulling on the stump with all the strength he could gather. He felt the stump rise, but it didn't give way. He clenched his teeth, grunting in effort as he pulled. His foot slipped and the stump sprung back into place.

Steve and Belinda had stopped shouting. Instead they stood in wide-eyed silence, watching Billy.

"Holy hell," Steve said.

"I think I can do this," Billy said. Facing away from the stump, Billy wrapped the chain around his waist and looped it up over one shoulder. "Hook me up."

Steve slipped the hook through the chain and gave it a tug. "Good luck, Buck."

Billy stepped forward, the chain tightening around his torso. The hoops bit into the skin on his belly, but he continued to advance. He leaned forward, digging his fingers into the lawn as he moved inch by inch, the stump creaking as it slowly rose behind him.

"You're doing it, Billy," Belinda said excitedly.

"Geeze-us," Steve said in amazement. "How much horsepower do you have in those legs?"

The stump let out a huge crack and Billy lurched forward half a foot. It hadn't given way just yet.

"Almost there, Billy," Steve said. "Good man."

Sweat pouring down his face, his teeth clenched tight, Billy continued pulling himself with his fingers, his legs shaking as they hauled against the force of the stump.

Then with a huge crack, the stump gave way. Billy stumbled forward a few steps and Belinda let out a scream of warning.

Billy whipped around to see the stump flying through the air at him. Instinctively, he lifted his hands and caught it, a shower of dirt spraying him in the face as it stopped, knocking Billy onto his butt. The stump was wider than him, and very, very heavy. Billy tilted forward and let the stump drop with a ground-shaking thump.

Billy stood, shrugged his shoulders and let the chain fall. He tugged the chain over his waist like he was removing a belt without unbuckling it. Dusting off his hands, Billy wiped the sweat from his head.

"Piece of cake," he panted.

Belinda and Steve stared at Billy, their faces pale.

"Where do you want it?" Billy tapped the stump with his boot.

"There is fine," Steve said.

Billy clapped his hands, ready for more action. *That was pretty fun.* "What next?"

"Um," Belinda said. "Now we need to dig up the grass that's been growing against the fence."

"Do you have another shovel?" Billy asked.

"In the garage," Belinda said.

Billy grabbed the shovel. When he returned to the backyard, Steve was digging a line. Billy followed, lifting clumps of grass between the line and the fence, and dumping them in the hole left by the stump.

The morning passed to afternoon quickly as they worked. Belinda made sandwiches and lemonade for lunch, Billy using the stump as a chair as he ate. Steve sat on a lawn chair, drinking a beer, and they talked baseball. He'd never really found something to talk with Steve about before. But the guy liked baseball. *Who knew?* And Steve was actually kind of funny. His commentary about the current players was pretty clever.

After lunch, Belinda pulled several crates of flowers from the garage. They spent the afternoon digging little holes and planting them. Belinda apparently knew a lot about flowers and spent most of the time explaining to Billy all the different types she'd picked and why. She loved flowers. Not just to look at, but to take care of. He hadn't talked to her about *stuff* before. Not stuff she was interested in. They'd never bonded the way Billy heard some kids do with their foster parents. He was in their home, and they fed him and clothed him. But he'd never spent time with her doing something she thought was cool. For the first time, Billy felt like he might be missing out on something when he moved out.

But if she can take care of flowers, why didn't she take care of me? Billy blinked back the sudden itch in his eye.

When they were done, Billy plopped down on the stump again to admire their work. It looked really, really good. The mulch was dark brown and followed the fence in an L shape from the back of the house to the side of the garage. Pink, white, purple, and red flowers popped with color in a zigzag pattern. The outside of the house was finally looking almost as neat as the insides.

Billy rubbed his thumb against his forefinger, feeling the dirt roll between his skin. "Looks great," he said.

Belinda stood beside him. She didn't respond so he looked up at her. Belinda nodded, her eyes brimming with tears. Billy had no idea how an afternoon of yard work could be so moving, but apparently it was.

"You know, Billy," Belinda said, her voice soft. "You turned out okay."

She patted him on the shoulder, and that's when it hit him. The emotion pouring from Belinda struck Billy like a train.

The feelings surged through his body, and he felt his throat hitch as tears formed in his eyes. Belinda was sad, so sad. She was devastated. Her heart was breaking as they rushed her into the emergency room. But she already knew it was too late, that little life inside hadn't quite made it.

Years later, she was fighting with Steve about it. About *her*. It was so long ago, but Steve and Belinda had never really stopped hurting.

Years before, when Belinda and Steve were still new, they sat in the doctor's office, looking at a chart about percentages of success. *'Have to sell the Pilot to pay for it,'* Steve had joked at the time. He had sold his car and she loved him for it.

And then there was the tiny pink shirt—a gift from her mom— she still kept in the shoebox in her closet; for when she needed to hold it and remember.

All those thoughts and feelings, the images, the smell of the anesthesia mask, had hit Billy in the split second her fingers touched his shoulder. He didn't see everything clearly, and he didn't understand any of what he saw. But he knew the pain she was in, even after all this time. And somehow it was connected to him—connected to her choice to foster. And how it stopped her from caring as much as she wanted to. She couldn't love him through the pain, even though she tried. As crappy as they had been, Billy understood for the first time, that Belinda was trying to be a good foster mom.

Billy's eyes were fixed on the flowers as he took in a breath, trying to calm the storm of misery welling inside him that wasn't even his. *I don't like feeling my own emotions, I* don't *need to feel someone else's.*

When Billy glanced up, he was alone. Belinda must have left at some point, but he hadn't even noticed. He wasn't even sure how long he'd sat there recovering from the emotional sucker punch.

Billy stood and made his way inside, his chest hurting like someone had just whacked him with a sledge hammer. And he was more tired than he should have been.

I knew when I signed up I was going to get powers from this. But hyperactive emotion reading just sucks.

He sat down at the formal dining room table, aware of his heart drumming in his chest. He stared at the next volume of the Essential Arcane resting on the table before him, not able to concentrate long enough to open it. As the minutes past, the pounding gradually grew softer.

When Mr. Fingers attacked him, he felt like someone had frappéd his brain. This was similar, but different, like someone had frappéd his heart. Mr. Fingers' assault made it hard to think. This made it hard to feel anything without aching.

A buzzing sound from somewhere outside made Billy start in surprise. He took a deep breath and rubbed his chest in an attempt to dull the phantom pain. Walking to the back room, he looked through the window to see what was causing the racket. Steve was in the backyard with a wood chipper he'd just rented. He was chopping off pieces of the stump with an axe and tossing them in. The chipper sprayed the side of the garage in blasts of wood chips, scattering sawdust all over the yard.

The Space Viking's Plight

EIGHTEEN MONTHS AFTER THE WELL

Queen Natalie dropped her robe behind her, revealing the thin shirt underneath, and gripped the oar again. The guards behind her murmured in surprise, and shifted uncomfortably, troubled that their queen would appear in public in such as state of undress. But these were not usual times.

"My lady," Natalie's husband Daniel said, surprise in his voice. She had not known he was close. "You . . . reveal much to your subjects this day."

Queen Natalie worked the oar, pulling with all her might. Though it was no usual oar. The handle spun a mighty wheel beside her; and through a mechanism of gears and pulleys, worked the oars extending from the ship into the infinite black. The motion moved the oars at an amazing speed. And coated with the metal the angel Gaeleon had forged that provided traction in the emptiness of the infinite black, multiplied by the thousands upon thousands of oars extending from the ship, it allowed them to travel faster than light itself.

And whilst the moonship was an amazing creation beyond any dream she had as a child—a bean-shaped moon, surrounded in a hull of wood, and rowed with magic oars through the infinite black— piloting them came at a price. The air inside was growing stale. The crops they had planted on the moon were not producing fruit and grains as they should have. Many rowers were falling ill, and at the risk of losing speed, the queen had stepped in to assist. It was hot work, too hot to be done while wearing the royal robes.

Queen Natalie exhaled as she pulled on the oar. "A leader helps where is needed, King Daniel."

"As you say," Daniel agreed in word only, not in his tone.

If they lost too much speed, their aim would be off. And according to the arithmetic of Gaeleon, if the speed of the moonships was not perfect, they would miss Earth entirely and find themselves travelling through the infinite black forever. While that thought did not appeal to Natalie, she wasn't sure it would make any difference. With so many rowers ill, they could not maintain the requisite speed for much longer.

As the sweat began to run down Natalie's back, she couldn't help but doubt her angelic counselor whom had set this journey in motion. Perhaps Gaeleon was wrong. Perhaps this mission to help William Blacksmith was ill-fated. Perhaps the angel they had counted as a friend had abandoned them, leaving her entire kingdom to flounder in the ocean of stars.

Natalie shook away the pessimism and rowed harder. There was no place for misgiving in a journey so perilous. Especially not from the queen that had led her people to this fate. Whatever this fate would end up being.

The other moonships fared better. On those vessels, it seemed the mechanisms orchestrated by the angel were functioning as expected. Their air was clearer, their food producing healthily. Though with only flashes of light to communicate between the ships, there was no way to ascertain the truthfulness of the reports. It may have been that they did not wish to concern their queen if they were in a similar plight. *More doubt,* she thought. She rowed harder.

Natalie felt her robe replaced on her shoulders. But she was hot and sweaty, too busy to be concerned with protocol. She shrugged it off.

"Please," Daniel said. "You must protect your modesty."

"Modesty is not important if we do not wish to endure eternity on this ship." She sucked in a breath and exhaled as she pulled. "I will row as needed to keep our course true. And I will do so as comfortably as possible."

"Natalie," Daniel said, his voice soft and worried.

Queen Natalie glared at her husband. He was not known for breaching etiquette, especially by acting so familiar in public. He understood it was their responsibility as the royal family to set an example, no matter how dire the situation became.

He looked back at her, a soft frown behind his beard, his eyes sad. He was a good man, and sincerely cared for the people. It was his gentle heart that made him unfit to be a leader, but made him a magnificent advisor. It was also why she loved him.

"Guard," Natalie called. "Row."

Without hesitation the guard took the queen's seat as she stood and continued rowing in her stead. The other guard had picked up her robe and handed it to Daniel. He draped it around Natalie's shoulders and she did not stop him.

"What is it, Daniel?" she asked confidentially. "You know we cannot afford to slow."

"Isaac is ill," he said simply.

"Continue until I return," Natalie ordered the guard. It was law that she must have two guards, but there had not been a single incident while they had been aboard the moonships. It was unlikely one would happen now.

"My Queen," the second guard said, not quite stepping in front of her. "You must have two guards watching you at all times."

Natalie groaned and approached the guard who rowed in her stead. She reached down and drew the sword from his hip. He glanced back in surprise at his queen, but he did not stop her. She handed the sword to Daniel.

"There, King of Phalon," she said to her husband. "You've been demoted to guard. Take me to our son."

Daniel gave her a soft smile, which faded immediately. He took her hand, another gesture which was too personal for the royal couple. His strong hand filled her with comfort, yet also granted her a sense of foreboding. *What has brought my strong husband to act as if all things are ending?*

They walked down the Glowerfine Path, the rowers to their right moving through their unending dance. A dozen rowers sat on each bench, a paddle in their hands, leaning forward and pulling back as a wheel as tall as a man spun next to them. Not a gear nor pulley had broken in the time they had rowed across the stars. Gaeleon had built them a good ship, the wooden parts persisting with more durability than she could have expected.

The grass growing on the side of the path, however, was not faring as well. The blades grew yellow and limp. The star light from the great windows above them simply was not enough to feed the plants, and the glowing stones that Gaeleon made had faded too quickly. That was not the case on the other moonships, their stones yet shone brightly, or so said the reports.

Queen Natalie arrived at the royal cottage and Daniel held open the door. The residence was miniscule compared to the castle Natalie grew up in, but in the months upon the moonship, it had felt more like home than the castle had. The royal duties on a small moon, where the chief responsibilities included eating and settling meaningless disputes, had left her a lot more time for being a mother; something which was all but absent from life upon Phalon. She had even learned Stone Battle and played it frequently with her sons. Seeing her sons laugh at a joke from Daniel somehow brought her more joy than them learning their letters, or passing a test from the sword master. She felt as if she was growing soft. Perhaps more time with her own father would have better prepared her for the duties of motherhood, rather than simply being raised to lead. It helped her understand Daniel better, and perhaps made her less prepared for what she knew she was walking into this night.

The Chief Healer, Lucinda, knelt beside the bed, waving scented smoke over Isaac's head. He was always a sweet boy and had grown much in his eleven years. One thing that could be said of her eldest son is that he always sincerely wished to help. Isaac's bones protruded from his elbows as he clutched his knees to his chest. His beautiful, thin face was now green and slick with sweat, as he shook violently with a snowchest. But none of that explained the smell in the house.

"What is that scent?" Natalie asked, her nose twitching in discomfort.

"Issac attempted to make stew with rotten groddish," Daniel explained. He gently nudged the healer aside and stooped next to the bed. "How do you feel, Isaac?" He brushed Isaac's sweat matted hair from his face.

Natalie watched her husband, wishing she knew what to do like he did; kneeling next to a sick child, the affection in his voice. They were all alien concepts to her, even after all these years of being a mother. It simply was not as natural as it seemed to be for some parents. Love came like breathing to them. She loved her sons, she did not doubt that. But she did not know how to express it. Not in the way Daniel did.

Isaac could not respond. He pressed his lips closed attempting to retain a retch.

"The groddish crop failed," Lucinda explained.

"Isaac was attempting to salvage what he could," Daniel added. "The rowers' families are . . ."

Natalie looked between her husband and the Chief Healer. "What?"

"My apologies, my queen," Lucinda said. "They are starving."

"What?" Panic as black as the infinite sky outside the moonships welled in Natalie's chest. "I knew food was scarce, but people are starving? Why did no one tell me?"

Lucinda fell to her knees, pressing her forehead to the floor. "We did not wish to trouble you. We wish to aid the Demonseed and believe in your mission. It was unthinkable that our whole civilization could perish in the infinite black. We could not accept it. It was not certain until the groddishes came up from the ground this morn."

Natalie looked at Daniel. "You knew?"

Daniel gave her a soft look. "We have been doing everything in our power to keep the people fed. But I am out of ideas. Isaac took it on himself to cook the rot out of the groddish. That is, as we can see, not an option."

"Stand, please," Natalie ordered Lucinda.

She stood, but kept her eyes on her toes.

"Will Isaac live?"

Lucinda pulled nervously at the smoking herbs in her hands. "Under normal circumstances, I would say yes. But without food it will be impossible for him to regain his strength. And it is only a matter of time before we all lose ours."

Natalie thought of the full breakfast she had enjoyed that morning and her stomach turned. Daniel's lack of appetite over the last few weeks suddenly made sense.

"How much food do we have left?" Natalie asked her husband. "Do not lie to me anymore. Do not obfuscate the truth under the pretense of protecting my feelings. How am I to lead if I do not understand the needs of my people?"

"The crop on the north underside bore some food."

"How much?" Natalie insisted.

Daniel gave her a sad look. "We can feed our ship for this evening."

"And then?"

"And then we will be eating the grass that lines the path."

"I understand," Natalie said. She stood for a long moment staring at her son in the throes of sickness. There was nothing she could do. She couldn't take him to the Shimmer Peak to watch the sunrise and feel the healing warmth of Phalon's sun. She would never see Shimmer Peak again, no Phalonians would. The doubt she had been suppressing for weeks flooded over her and she placed a hand on the doorway to keep from falling to the floor.

I have doomed my kingdom, my civilization, to a death unimaginable. We will starve out here. Someday our ships, piloted by our skeletons will find a path around some sun and become true moons. My father would be sore displeased with me. If he could see me. That thought hit Natalie with such a weight she almost lost all strength. She tightened her grip on the doorframe. *What if my father cannot see me out here? Is his spirit still on Phalon, wandering his empty castle, alone and bewildered?*

In response, she heard a ghostly cry in her ears and she knew that her father regretted choosing her. Her knees wavered and Daniel took her hand. It was all that kept her on her feet.

But then she heard the ghostly cry again.

"What is that?" Daniel asked, peering through the window of the cottage.

Natalie lifted her head, hearing a sound that she had not heard before. A commotion arose on the moonship. People were calling, shouting. The sound was confused, excited, and panicked, all at once.

Natalie ran from the house to see families standing on the paths between the cottages, pointing towards the great window above them. The rowers remained in their seats, as they should, but as one they all looked over their shoulders and up into the infinite black.

"It's a sword," someone called.

"It glows with the fire of a sun," someone else shouted.

"It flies with us," another said. "Faster than light itself."

Natalie ran forward until she could peer through the great window above her. For the first time since they had left Phalon, she saw something beyond the glass other than starlight.

It was indeed a sword, cutting through space easily. It must have been a moonship, too, Natalie supposed. But it had no oars reaching into space. A fire glowed from the hilt. Lights glittered along the length of the blade and she felt like she was looking out from the castle tower at the firelights of a city glittering below her, or perhaps the reflection of the setting sun in a river.

The sword grew in size. It was approaching the moonship, but against the backdrop of stars, she had no way to gauge its actual size. It continued to grow as it approached, until it filled the whole of the great window. The sword burned through space, much larger than any of her moonships, and despite the absence of oars, was much faster.

"There are more!" a child shouted.

Natalie turned. Through the other great window, far across the moonship, she glimpsed more swords as they cut across the stars, matching the speed of the moonships. Natalie dropped her robe behind her and sprinted down the Glowerfine path. Despite being short of breath, she climbed the stairs to the black bridge two at a time.

When she burst through the door the soldier standing sentinel was unmoving, staring at the sight surrounding them.

Hundreds of swords encircled her fleet of moonships, glowing yellow and blue and green, their hilts aflame as they sliced through the infinite black. Each sword had picked a moonship and matched its speed as it slowly moved closer.

"Are we under attack?" the solder asked, his voice small, his hand on his own sword. "Pirates from the stars?"

"No," Queen Natalie said, a smile breaking over her face. "Those are moonships from another planet here to aid us in our plight." Her soul rejoiced at the sight. They would not starve. Her rowers could be healed. Isaac would recover to try another foolish experiment in an attempt to help. Natalie touched the glass between her and the infinite black, her heart full of joy and a prayer of thanks to the Gods of Phalon. "Our angel Gaeleon has not forgotten us."

The Demøn Who
Søught Løve

Aldergaben, the demon who would become known as the
Patriarch, enjoyed the stares of his fellow demons as he rode
through the forging fields, the carriage pulled by a dozen
huge bulfeghow. The anvils chimed around them as his servants
worked the sapphyril, forging swords and arrows for his brother,
Aberdem. His maid sat beside him, holding his hand and leaning into
his arm as they rode. He knew what a sight they were. His towering
frame contrast against her human form. He cared not for the opinions
of other demons. They were nothing compared to him. But more than
that, he loved his maid. With love burning in his heart there was
nothing any demon could say to him that would darken his mind.

Though something that did concern him were the looks cast in
the direction of their child. Their son stood at the front of the carriage,
watching the bulfeghow pulling at the reigns, letting out squeals of
delight. The demons surrounding them eyed his child with fear, or
hunger. He was by all rights an abomination, a union of the Human

and Demonic Realms. Slay him or eat him, all who saw him wished to kill the half-demon. Yet as Aldergaben had found love in his human maid, what surprised him was the multiplication of love as their family grew. He had more love now they had a child to share it with. And with it, more fear for their safety.

It was a short ride across the forging fields to the castle of Melferim, his sister. Her castle was set atop a hill, the towers tall, sharp, and thin as needles. The stairwells were smooth to allow her to slither comfortably about her domain. Forged of deep grey stone, the castle glistened majestically against the purple sky, surrounded by a skillfully manicured garden of every green plant a demon could find in the realm.

She slithered through the grand doorway as they arrived, greeting Aldergaben and his human in the yard, immensely pleased to see her brother, as always. She rose on her snake tail to look her brother in the eye and embraced him.

Melferim had not scorned Aldergaben for his human as all other demons had. Indeed, she had found the situation amusing, even fascinating. She often asked his maid numerous questions when they met, inquiring of her about all facets of human life, of their food, their likes, their celebrations and times of mourning. And especially of the unusual concept of love.

"Oh my. Am I honored by the presence of a god?" Melferim exclaimed when she saw her brother, joking of the title Aldergaben had recently earned.

Aldergaben laughed. "Bah, you will soon earn the epithet yourself."

"I'm not sure I want it," Melferim replied. "The God of Bats suits you. It was your fate to become so. Aberdem, however, has been nauseating since he became a god. I should shun the title just to spite him."

Aldergaben found the smile on his lips fading. Their brother was not like them. He took great offence to even petty slights.

"Fear not," Melferim said gently. "I'll earn it. Godhood has certain benefits that I would like to employ myself. Come, the servants are setting our meal in the garden."

She led them through an arch of blooming rownknife, a tribe of pixies flittered around the plants, harvesting the sap. In the perfectly manicured garden before them, spidermaids laid the meal on a small table. Aldergaben recognized the fare as biscuits and tea.

The dining area was set atop a cliff overlooking the forging fields. Aldergaben felt great satisfaction watching his demons working the anvils. He would have the swords for his brother's army ahead of schedule. His wife placed their child on the grass and little half-demon immediately toddled off to chase the pixies, laughing in delight as he did.

"He is the most joy-filled demonling I have ever beheld," mused Melferim.

"He has the love of a mother," the Patriarch replied, a smile on his face as he watched his son play. "Perhaps more love would benefit the realm of demons."

Melferim laughed and directed them to sit at the table. Quite used to demon accommodations, his wife pulled herself up to the seat set out for her and knelt on it so she could see over the table. The table suddenly appeared huge in his eyes next to his petite human. He had lived for a thousand thousand turns, and thought he knew all, but the gift his wife had given him, without knowing, was the gift of seeing things anew through another's eyes.

Once seated, Melferim immediately turned to his maid. "Tell me once more," she said. "I am yet to comprehend why you would choose my brother over all humans and demons to bear a child with."

His wife took up a biscuit and broke it in two. She took a bite and smiled at the taste. "Your cooking has improved, Melferim."

"Thank you," she replied. "But please, answer my question. I simply cannot understand."

"Love is impossible to explain," the human replied. "It is something you must experience. Aldergaben has proven to me that his mind is of great worth. He is clever, his choice of words make me laugh. He is a good leader. The demons that work the forges are compensated for their craft. Their complaints are listened to and addressed where possible."

"And these things make you love him?" Melferim asked.

"They incline my mind towards him," the maid said. "But it is his heart in which I find the most value."

Aldergaben sipped the tea as he listened, his mouth puckering at the peculiar, yet not unpleasant, taste. "What is this?"

"Lemon tea," Melferim replied.

"Most odd." Aldergaben sipped again.

"How so?" Melferim insisted. "How can you see what is in the heart?"

His wife smiled and touched his hand. "The heart is expressed in all his actions. And his actions are kind, and good. He cares for others as I have seen no creature do. And for that I love him."

"Kind and good?" Melferim laughed. "Do not let our elder brother hear that."

"It is too late for that," a voice boomed from beyond the castle. Aberdem, the God of Dragons, appeared in the sky, flapping his wings once to halt his movement, he landed beside the table. He was the biggest demon in all the Demonic Realm. A dragon of great length, his wings as broad as a mountain, his scales red as the human sun, and harder than sapphyril. He could not hope to fit more than his head in the front door of Melferim's castle. "You forget I can hear long before I am seen."

Aldergaben stood. "Aberdem, come join us. We are eating biscuits."

"What in the depths is a biscuits?" Aberdem said, eyeing the table beneath him with disgust.

"A human confection," Aldergaben said. "My wife has made them for us," he lied.

Aberdem scoffed. "The only confection I see here is this human. I will gladly eat her and end your distraction."

The maid smiled, but moved slightly lower, hiding behind the table. Aldergaben was a big demon, but Aberdem was certainly far bigger.

"What good is she?" Aberdem asked. "Does she play music? Music enlivens the mind. Fetch her a harp and make her useful at least."

"The human is mine," Aldergaben reminded his brother. "You are not to touch her. But you may have as many biscuits as you wish."

"I do not need biscuits, I am here to know where my swords are. The army is in need of fresh armaments and you are falling behind."

Aldergaben kept the frustration out of his voice. Growing up with a being such as Aberdem had taught him to conceal his emotions when needed. "I am on schedule, Abby, and you are aware of that. You are simply unhappy with how I choose to spend my free time."

"We are at war. There is no such thing as free time." Aberdem growled. "I am the God of Dragons, and when I see something amiss I aim to correct it."

Aldergaben resisted scoffing. Aberdem did enjoy reminding them of his title. "You are no god of mine," Aldergaben said, a laugh in his voice. "You are my elder brother. I forge weapons to the end of annihilating humans, but I do not hail to you."

Aberdem snarled at the maid. "If you wish to see the end of humans, then kill this one here and be that much closer to our goal."

"She was gifted to me by you to do as I wish. I *am* doing as I wish. You will not take my agency, will you?"

"Free will, unchecked, is chaos," Aberdem said. "Galler," he called.

A dragon whom Aldergaben had not noticed came forward from behind Aberdem's leg. He was much smaller, shorter than

Aldergaben. His scales were emerald, and his nose too short to be considered a handsome dragon. But he possessed the most valuable trait for an assistant of Aberdem—he thought the God of Dragons was perfect. In his claws, Galler held a familiar sword which he handed to Aldergaben.

"Sinewol," Aldergaben said the sword's name. He drew the blade from its sheath and knew immediately why Aberdem was returning the sword. It was dull, the metal peppered with nicks.

Aberdem snarled. "My grand general cannot have his blade looking as such after only killing a thousand humans."

"This is disappointing," Aldergaben agreed. "It would appear the magic weakened the sapphyril."

"You claim to have free time and yet you send me inferior weapons?" Aberdem said. "I expect more from you."

"As do I." Aldergaben nodded. "This is Kolan's work. He is no longer in my employ."

"For truth?" Aberdem asked. "I liked his attitude. I thought he had potential."

Aldergaben glanced at his maid. She knew where Kolan had gone. And why.

"Yes, I can see why you two got along so well," Aldergaben said. "I'll forge your grand general another, greater sword."

"Why not have your apprentice do it?"

"I am currently without an apprentice."

Aberdem scoffed. "The God of Bats, the greatest forge master in all three realms, and you have no apprentice? You do not care for my success in the war against humans, do you? All you care for is your pet human. She is a distraction and a weakness."

"Aberdem," Melferim said as she stood, taking her brother by the leg and leading him away from their supper. "Listen to the ringing of the anvils across the forging fields. Is that not music? Aldergaben has never let you down. He rules his demesnes with order and an iron soul. Much as you lead your armies. Your will is strong, your purpose pure. There has never been such an army in all eternity as the one you command. With such strength of will and might, you will not fail. With your brother's armaments, you shall be victorious. Fear not his little toy. He will tire of her soon and eat her, or throw her into the rivers of reality that flow beneath our feet."

Aberdem nodded. "My army is unstoppable despite our brother's less than adept performance. Even without weapons, the humans cannot stand against us, if it comes to it. And what of your crops?"

Melferim smiled. "The harvest was bountiful. The carriages of grain and salted spider are already on their way to your forces. They will be fed a turn before you requested it."

The spidermaids who waited on them shuddered at the news. Aldergaben couldn't help but notice the spider's reaction. Something that would have, once, never occurred to him. *I see through my wife's eyes,* he thought.

"Very good," Aberdem said. "You have always pleased me, my little snake."

"With such a mighty big brother to look up to, I have wanted nothing but to earn your favor."

"You have, Melferim." He turned his back on Aldergaben and spoke quietly. "Though I do worry about Aldergaben. He is too comfortable with his human. Allowing her to ride in his carriage as if she is a concubine. And that child of theirs is odd indeed. It lacks horns as he does. Other than its skin and wings, he looks almost human."

"Their child is nothing to be concerned about," she whispered. "I will see that he grows loyal to purpose of the Demonic Realm and the God of Dragons."

"I trust you will," Aberdem said. "Get me the swords tonight," he called as he flapped his wings and rose into the purple. "You have half a turn to replace the rubbish you forged for my grand general."

The child stopped chasing sprites for a moment to watch his uncle soar away, with Galler close behind.

"Did you hear that?" Melferim asked as she returned to the table.

"Every word," Aldergaben replied. "He forgets that I also have great hearing. But we must return. Apparently, we have a turn of forging to do by this evening. Thank you for a lovely afternoon."

The maid climbed down from the demon-sized chair and curtseyed to Melferim. "Thank you for your hospitality. Your cooking is wonderful. These taste just like the biscuits my mother would make." A moment of sadness passed over his maid. She did not often mention her family, and avoided speaking of them.

"Thank you for teaching me," Melferim replied. "I look forward to learning more human dishes."

The maid called after her son. In response, he laughed loudly and ran away to hide behind the bushes. She gave chase, the demonling chortling as his mother snatched him up. She kissed him on the head and pinched the tips of his wings, which set him into a fit of giggles. Aldergaben and Melferim stood beside one other, watching the motherly show of affection that was so alien to them both.

"Until next time," Aldergaben said as he walked through the rownknife arch and back to his carriage.

Many turns passed in which Aldergaben provided swords and arrows to the demonic armies. He reforged Sinewol himself. There simply was no apprentice up to the task. Kolan had poured so much magic into the blade that there was little holding the sapphyril together. One of Kolan's greatest failings was his lack of restraint, which made him both useless and dangerous. Imprisoning him was the only option.

When Aldergaben delivered the weapons to his brother, he could not help but notice the expression of his wife. With each delivery, the action grew harder. These weapons were for the express purpose of slaughtering humans. And with each human killed, his maid grew more alone.

One morn, there came a knock at the door. Aldergaben, who sat at breakfast, placed his meat down and called, "Come."

A footdemon entered. "The goddess Melferim," he announced.

Aldergaben stood as his sister slithered into the chamber.

"Behold," Melferim exclaimed, excitement painted in her features "I have found love for myself."

"That's wonderful," the maid said from her seat at the table.

Behind Melferim, a human staggered into the chamber. The man appeared terrified. He glanced up at Melferim with a wan expression, his legs seeming barely to hold up his weight. His gaze caught the maid, confusion crossing his face, then pleading.

"Come." The maid climbed down from her place at the table and approached the newcomer. "What is your name?"

"I am Helman," he said weakly.

"Come, Helman, I'm sure your day has been full of surprises. Let me show you where you can clean and get a new change of clothes."

"What?" he replied.

"Come with me," the maid said. "You shall be fine."

The maid led Helman from the chamber into the washrooms. Once out of sight, Aldergaben heard Helman explode with questions.

"Where did you find your love?" Aldergaben asked his sister.

"I took him from the captives of Aberdem's last pillaging. I found him most pleasing to my eyes out of all the humans."

"Is he indeed your love?" Aldergaben asked.

Melferim shrugged. "I wish for him to be. Though I still do not understand what love is."

"How long has he been with you?"

"Two days."

"Give it time. It took much longer than a dozen turns for my love to grow."

"How will I know it when it comes? How will I recognize it?" She looked around as if love might be floating above her head in a cloud.

"Love is within. Love simply is," Aldergaben explained. "It is the desire to care for her more than the desire to care for yourself. It is selfless. It distracts you from your duties as you consider their needs."

"You make love sound inconvenient."

Aldergaben smiled broadly. "It is the most wonderful inconvenience I have ever experienced."

"I hope to experience it. My Helman seems a good human."

The Patriarch did not say what was in his heart. Falling in love with his maid was serendipitous. He did not think that love was as simple as picking a human. It was a case of the universe aligning and the light from the depths glowing through all existence. But he wished the best for his sister.

Melferim kept Helman at her castle for many turns. He was always happy to see the maid and sought a private audience with her whenever she visited. However, Helman never expressed joy at his time with Melferim. His maid told Aldergaben that, on more than one occasion, Helman suggested the maid flee with him back to the Human Realm. But she loved Aldergaben, and did not wish to leave. Living with and loving a demon was a situation which Helman could not comprehend.

After many more turns, Melferim fell pregnant with the human's child. Aberdem was away at war at this time, taking the lands across the human oceans. Word must have reached him of the pregnancy, for a decree went out across all the Demonic Realm: Anything not demon within the Demonic Realm must be slain.

Nothing happened to Aldergaben's wife and child of course. It would be madness for any demon to slay the family of a god. But Aldergaben did worry that his sister would bend to the will of their elder brother. He feared for the unborn child.

Melferim expressed to Aldergaben a hope that the babe would increase the love which the human had for her, as it seemed to do with his family. When the time for the birth came, Aldergaben waited outside in the hall with Helman. The human's face was not the face of a man looking forward to the birth of his child—he was afraid. He did not wish to be a father, especially not to a child born of a union between the Earthly and Demonic Realms.

The time came for them to enter and see Melferim's son. Aldergaben followed Helman into the chamber, hand in hand with his maid. Melferim cradled her minutes-old child, singing softly. The babe slept against her chest, looking at peace with all existence. Aldergaben felt the love grow inside him that day as he beheld his beautiful nephew.

Helman, on the other hand, let out a moan of horror. "My son is a demon," he said, stumbling away from the sight before him. "An abomination. Surely I am cursed for this unholy alliance."

"An abomination?" Melferim asked. "This child is an abomination in your eyes?"

"He is hideous," Helman exclaimed as he pressed against the wall, his eyes wide, his mouth drawn in horror. "God has forsaken me. I am doomed."

Melferim ran a finger down the child's chest, seeming amazed at the life in her arms. "Helman, in all our time together, have you grown to love me?"

Helman hesitated, looking at Melferim with tears on his fearful face. "No. I do not love you. I never have."

"You may leave," she said simply.

"What?" Helman asked.

"Leave," Melferim said. "You are no longer a captive here. Return to the Human Realm to do as you will."

Helman seemed struck dumb. "For truth?" he stammered finally.

"For truth. I do not love you either. You have been a disappointment."

Without another word, Helman fled from the chamber. Aldergaben never saw the human again. He doubted the human made it further than the gate of the castle. The forging field held a hundred thousand demons, all with hammers at hand. And forging was hungry work.

"I am sorry you did not find love," Aldergaben said, placing a hand on the child's head.

Melferim smiled. "My Helman was a disappointment," she said. "But he was not entirely useless."

"How so?" the maid asked.

Melferim held up her son and kissed his cheek. "I have found the love I sought, and I find it in my child. My heart is full of a desire to protect him, to serve him, to give him all I have."

"Family should bring an increase of love," the maid said, stroking the sleeping demon's face. "You are right in that."

"What shall you call my nephew?" Aldergaben asked.

"His name will be Corthas."

The Sides We Chøøse

TWO WEEKS AFTER THE WELL

"Belle," her mom screeched. "Door."

"I'm busy," Belle called back. Nobody came to visit her anyway. It couldn't be anyone important.

Belle didn't look up from the soldering iron in her hands as she attached the wire to the detonator. This one was going to be good. The rocket she was making would pick a target and stay locked on, like a sucker-seeking missile. It was dangerous work, but that's what made it so exciting. She wiped a bead of sweat from her shaved scalp and continued working.

"Ma'am," an unfamiliar voice said from behind her as the door creaked open.

She dropped the soldering iron and reached for the gun hiding in the backpack by her foot, but she wasn't fast enough. The intruder kicked the bag away from her hand and shoved her back into her seat.

"Don't think about it," the intruder said, taking a cautious step back. "Put up your hands."

Belle turned slowly to see a cop standing over her. The cop was an average height and in good shape, the name Dillan sewn on her chest. She gripped a bright yellow stun gun, aimed at Belle's face. Five more cops were crowded together in the small hall of their trailer behind her, each with their gun drawn.

"What did you do, Belle?" her mom barked. She shoved past the cops and into the room, ignoring the guns. Belle's mom was skinny, wearing nothing but a tank top and jeans with gashes all the way up to her hips. She held a cigarette between her fingers and slapped Belle across the back of the head with her free hand. "What did you do? Huh? Why are the cops here with guns? Huh?"

"Ma'am," the cop said. "Ma'am, we're trying to arrest her. Please step away."

"Yeah?" Belle lunged for the button rigged up under her desk, just in case someone showed up like this. She wasn't fast enough.

The gun went off and Belle's body became rigid, a burning pain freezing every single muscle.

Son of a . . . Belle thought disjointedly as she toppled off her chair and slumped onto the floor.

The next two minutes were a blur. She heard her mom yelling, she felt herself slammed onto her stomach as her hands were cuffed behind her back. Two of the cops picked her up by the arms and dragged her through the trailer and down the steps. She twisted her head, her mom was framed in the door of the trailer, screaming at an officer as he blocked her way.

"Hey," Belle shouted, her mouth finally working again. "Aren't you going to read me my rights?"

The cops holding her laughed and dumped her on the road behind the police cruiser. For the first time ever, Belle wished they lived on a busier street so some jackass with a cell phone could film the police brutality. The neighbor's trailers were blocked by thick brush; they wouldn't be able to see what these jerks were doing to her.

She looked back at her mom, who was trying to shove the cop out of the way. He lifted his stun gun and zapped her, too.

Shoving cops gets you shot, Mom, Belle thought.

Then the cop kicked her rigid form through the door and slammed it shut.

What the hell? Belle pushed herself up with her cuffed hands as officer Dillan approached. "You guys are not very professional," she yelled up at her.

Officer Dillan planted a boot in Belle's stomach and she doubled over in pain.

Dillan squatted down next to her, she grabbed Belle by the chin and waved her stun gun in her face. "Knock it off or you get zapped again."

Belle cracked her forehead into the cop's nose. Dillan recoiled, swearing in pain. She refocused and socked Belle across the jaw. Belle flew back, whacking her head against the road. There was more laughter from the officers.

Through the pain, she heard the trunk of the police cruiser open and watched helplessly as she was flung in the back.

"I'm beginning to think you guys aren't cops," she shouted.

"You need to shut up." Dillan pointed her stun gun at Belle again and pulled the trigger.

Belle convulsed, cracking her knees into the spare tire. Laughing, Dillan slammed the trunk closed. Seconds later, the car was moving. Belle had a feeling they weren't going to the police station, but her body hurt too much to keep track of what happened next. The pain in her stomach, her head, and all her muscles felt like a black fog rolling over her consciousness.

Belle woke up, and for a second thought she was still in the trunk. She couldn't see a damn thing. Blinking, she focused on the darkness around her. Some kind of bag had been pulled over her head. Shadowy figures moved on the outside, there was no way to tell who they were or what they wanted. But she knew her breathing was giving her fear away, it was short and rapid, laced with tears threatening to come.

But then she noticed something digging into her wrists. *I'm freaking tied up,* she realized. The ropes tore against her skin as she strained against the restraints. Her thighs and ankles ached where more chords bit into them, binding her to some hard, wooden chair. She had no idea how long she'd been bound, but her hands were numb, her feet throbbed. Fighting down the urge to start hollering, Belle took a deep breath; *I have to figure out what's going on first.*

If the people who had kidnapped her just showed their faces, she could stare them down. But without that, she was just a girl with a bag on her head; afraid, and not a threat.

A light was shining somewhere close by, but she couldn't make anything out. Voices talked quietly beyond the light. They sounded too calm, like this was a situation they knew so well they were almost bored with it. Belle had never been in a position this bad, and didn't want to let it show, but she was failing. Life had kicked her down again and again, and she knew how to stand up to it.

But being tied up, utterly helpless, was more overwhelming than she could have imagined. She was lost. What had happened to her mom? Was anyone going to care she was gone? Without meaning to, Belle gasped in a pitiful breath.

No. Don't. Don't let it get to you. Don't be weak. Don't, she ordered herself. But the tears were going to come, and she couldn't stop them.

Someone up there had mercy on her. Seconds before she totally lost it, a voice beyond the light made a decision and she heard footsteps approach. The bag lifted from her head and she breathed in sharply. Her eyes stung in the sudden brightness and she squeezed them shut until the sensation passed.

Free from the bag, Belle took in as much as she could, just in case they jacked her ability to see again. She was in some kind of warehouse. The air was chilly and she shuddered, goosebumps forming across her scalp. Three yards away was a table, a lamp—the only source of light in the huge room—was set upon it. She could make out the faint outlines of steel girders above her, but she couldn't see the walls. A dozen large figures stood in the shadows, watching her. The darkness hid their faces, but not the HKs in their hands.

In front of the table stood Dillan, looking freaking pleased with herself, a hand resting on the real gun at her hip.

Beside the table in a comfortable looking armchair, sat a bald man, his chest and biceps stretching an expensive-ass suit. He was nonchalantly shaking a bottle of brown liquid in his hand as he watched Belle, an impassive expression on his face. He popped open the lid and took a swig. A flash of red glinted from his eyes and she suddenly knew who he was.

"Marcus Blood," Belle said. She'd never thought twice about the guy before. But now she wanted nothing more than to jam his protein shaker down his throat. She flexed, trying to stand, but she didn't move at all. "What the hell do you want?"

"Good evening, Belle," Blood said, capping his drink and shaking it once more. He indicated the cop behind him. "I understand Officer Dillan was rougher than I would have liked and for that I apologize. I assure you our first meeting was intended to be far more cordial."

Belle let out a loud, humorless laugh. "Sure, that's why you have a kidnapping warehouse with a chair ready to go. I'm not a freaking moron."

Blood inclined his head. "You are certainly not, which is why we are having this conversation."

"What do you want?" Belle gripped the arms of the chair, straining to find some give in the ropes.

Blood sighed, smirking. "Let's get to the point. Do you know what I do?"

"Besides kidnapping people and tying them up? You sell knockoff jewelry or something."

Anger appeared in the corners of his blood-stained eyes for a moment. That made Belle smile. *This guy takes his necklaces seriously.*

"Not quite," Blood said coolly. "I find the finest gems this planet has forged, and I craft them into works of art for which people pay millions of dollars."

"What does that crap have to do with me being tied to a freaking chair?" she shouted the last words, tugging on the ropes. The chair scraped across the floor an inch, the sound echoing through the warehouse.

Blood sipped his protein drink and smacked his lips. "I'm an artist at heart. I design the pieces myself. It was a hobby that bloomed into an obsession."

"I want my lawyer," Belle demanded.

Blood chuckled. "No, you won't be getting a lawyer. You're poor; one of the failsafes built into this great country. The poor are not protected from the law like the best of us. It helps keep the masses where we want them. Besides, you're not under arrest."

"Then let me go."

Blood placed his drink on the table and leaned forward, his palms pressed together. "I'm not quite sure you're grasping the gravity of this situation. You're not free to leave either."

"Then get it over with," she screamed. She glanced at the shadows behind Blood. She'd been in this kind of position before. Never this bad. But she knew what was coming.

Blood stood, buttoning up one button on his suit coat. "I think you misunderstand. You're here as my special guest."

"Oh, this is a great honor," Belle spat. "Thank you." She desperately wanted to break free just to slap that stupid smile off his face.

Blood smirked. "Though we just met, I understand you well enough to know you would have never come on your own. And I insist you hear me out."

"You're not giving me a choice."

"When I have something worth saying, I love a captive audience." He chuckled at the pun.

Belle stared at him. People usually cringed away from her whenever she made eye contact. The bald head, the tattoos, and her physique was enough to intimidate most people. Blood didn't seem to care at all. "You're freaking hilarious. Get to the point."

Blood held his hands out wide. "Though you can't see it, you are on the precipice of a grand opportunity. Another great thing about this country is that you can earn wealth, if you're *worthy*." He started sounding like an annoying high school teacher, so full of themselves thinking they know so much. "One can be worthy if you're good at a sport, or particularly skilled at that game called 'business'. Or, on occasion, if you're an artist, like me, you can reap the riches available to those who are able to take them. You're an artist, too, Belle." Blood approached Belle as he talked, sounding like some loser salesman.

Belle didn't break eye contact with him. "What are you talking about? I'm not a stupid artist. I haven't painted a damn thing in my life."

"Oh, but you have," Blood spoke like he was revealing a great secret.

He walked back to the table and picked up a charred piece of wood, half an inch thick and about the size of a high school locker door. She hadn't seen it lying on the table. He held it up to the light and Belle recognized it immediately. It was the backing board she'd mounted the bomb on—the bomb she'd made to kill Ash-Lea Grey.

"I can see you recognize it. This is a work of art," Blood said appreciatively, turning the wood over in his hands.

Belle shook her head in confusion. "How the hell did you get that? Why did you get that? It's not art, it's just a bomb. I can make those in my sleep."

"I'm sure you can." Blood laughed to himself. "The specific directional blast you were able to create using these simple components is remarkable. Honestly, it's prodigious. This piece of wood survived the blast. And the explosive power was exponentially more than you'd expect from the amount of propellant used. My experts aren't sure how you created so much force with so little material."

"You didn't answer any of my questions." This guy was being so freaking annoying. "So what if your guys don't know what I did?"

Blood made a pleased chuckle. "That's my point. You worked magic with this, Belle."

Belle was growing more confused by the moment. If they weren't going to hurt her, why was she tied up? And why did Marcus Blood give a crap about a bomb she'd made? She'd been screwing with explosives since she was a kid. The locker bomb was nothing special like he made it sound. They must have been after something; but she had nothing, except a reference from her manager at Taco Tuesdays, nothing a guy as rich as Blood would want. "You trying to butter me up?"

"I am." Blood sipped his shake. "You have potential, Belle. But you're also stupid."

"You suck at flirting," Belle retorted. "And I don't just mean tying me up."

Blood looked her up and down, a smile on his lips, but not a sleazy one. "I appreciate that you can still utilize humor when you're as scared as you are. You don't know this yet, but that's the essence of bravery. I'm feeling better about choosing you every minute."

"Even though I'm stupid?" she said.

"Yes. You're very green. But that's something in which I hope I'm able to assist you."

The faceless guards with guns still stood in the shadows, too afraid to show themselves. Dillan hadn't moved the entire time they talked. She looked on, smiling sadistically as she watched Belle squirm. *First chance I get I'm going to beat that smile off her face.*

Blood cleared his throat. "Your first problem is that we tracked you down with the gum you used to seal the locker door shut. That was worse than an amateur mistake—that was idiotic. You must swallow your juvenile pride if you wish to work with me."

"Work with you?" Belle scoffed. "You want me to make you a taco? I don't know how to do anything."

Blood gave a sympathetic frown. "I make it a point to understand as much as I can about the people with whom I plan to work. I know where you come from and I understand you didn't get much encouragement as you grew. I know your mother is . . . not up to the task of being a mother. And your father. Well, we weren't quite able to locate him either."

That cut too deep. It didn't matter how much money this guy had, he didn't get to start digging into Belle's family and throwing it in her face. "What do you want with me?" she bellowed.

Blood knelt beside Belle and put a hand on her shoulder. He had huge hands. When he spoke, it was in a soft voice; kind of deep and soothing. "I'm here to give you that encouragement. Because you are a fine artist. You simply need to receive the correct tutelage and I feel you will accomplish incredible things." He straightened and gestured into the shadows beyond the table. "I'd like you to meet my associate. It was on her recommendation that I'm offering you this position."

A shadow started to move from the back of the warehouse. Belle had thought that it was a stack of boxes or something, but it started walking towards them. The looming figure stepped into the light, bigger than Belle could have imagined. The *thing* had to be at least twelve feet tall, with grey skin, and a black robe wrapped around a vaguely feminine body.

Belle bit back the urge to scream as she flinched away from the monster, trying desperately to pull herself free from the ropes. She thought she could show her bravery by staring the kidnappers in the face. But there was no way in hell she could keep her cool with a surprise like this. Whatever they had planned for her, she prayed it didn't include that thing.

"It's going to be okay, Belle. We're not going to hurt you," Blood said in a reassuring voice. "This is my associate, Galberon. She's . . . not from around here, as you can see."

"Where is she from?" Belle asked, pressing back into the chair as far as she could go.

"She's a demon. Their plane of existence is called the Demonic Realm."

"Stonevale," Galberon stated, her voice cavernous, without inflection.

"Ah," Blood replied, amused. "She's from Stonevale, here as a consultant. We have some upcoming projects that we need some assistance with and Galberon is not able to work like she used to."

The monster held up her arms. Where her forearms should have been were two stumps with jagged hooks strapped to the ends.

"Galberon was in an accident," Blood explained. "And because of some demonic technicality which I don't understand, she can't get her hands back just yet. So we need someone to help her out, and perhaps learn something along the way. We'd like that someone to be you."

Belle couldn't tear her eyes away from the demon. It simply stood there watching her. But in her black eyes, Belle could see a deep intelligence. Galberon wasn't a mindless Frankenstein, she was clever, and dangerous. A flicker of excitement shivered through Belle's chest.

"So, how's it going, Galberon?" Belle asked.

"Girl," Galberon replied in greeting.

"Don't take it personally," Blood said. "Galberon doesn't trouble herself by learning human names."

"There are too many," Galberon explained. "So you're Girl."

"I . . . I don't understand what you want from me," Belle said through shaking lips.

Blood smiled as he watched Belle trying to not freak out. "You are an artist, Belle, but Galberon is Mozart. She is Michelangelo—and she can teach you to be, too. If you would stop being so obstinate and listen to what I'm offering."

"Why should I help you?" Belle said, her voice sounding weak to herself.

"If you don't, Officer Dillan will take you to the station where you will be processed for attempted murder, and several other charges. This evidence here," he held up the backer, "is covered in your clumsy fingerprints. And as I pointed out, you will not have a decent lawyer to assist you with that process. But if you do agree to work with me, I will allow you a fair cut of the several trillion dollars this job will pay."

Belle's brain stopped processing for a moment. "Trillion?"

"Yes. I'm being paid several," he spaced out the words letting Belle absorb them, "trillion dollars. I'm going to be the richest man to have ever lived. Now isn't that something?"

It took ten seconds before Belle's mouth worked again. "How . . . how much are we talking? For me?"

"I'm sure I could spare a few million for you." He spoke casually, like he was deciding who got the leftover taco. "If everything goes according to plan."

"Million?" Belle swallowed.

"Not just that, but I will provide you with resources to ensure you understand how to invest it invisibly, so you will not be noticed by the authorities. You'll be able to live the rest of your life in luxury you have only dreamed about."

Money would solve almost every single problem Belle could come up with. *But I don't need money. I've been fine without it up until now.* "What if I don't just want money?"

Blood laughed. "Everyone wants money. What else is there?"

"I want a job. For good."

Blood smiled, and for the first time it reached his bloody eyes. "I'm certain I can find a place for you in my enterprises."

The thought of being a part of something was more exciting than the money. She would get to work with people, skilled people, who knew what they were doing; who respected it when someone did a good freaking job. "I know how to be a team player."

He indicated the dozens of figures standing in the shadows behind him. "Belle, you will be the star player on a very elite team, doing some very exciting work. Much more exciting than playing in some major league baseball game. And far more lucrative."

Belle nodded. Behind Blood, Dillan continued to stand, watching the conversation in silence; though now her eyes were fixed on Galberon, a distinct disgust in them. If Dillan hated Galberon, that made Belle like the demon that much more. If she worked with Blood, she could pay Dillan back for the bruises, as soon as the opportunity came along.

Galberon walked forward and with a flick of her hooks, cut the ropes around Belle's wrists and legs.

Belle smiled up at the demon, her heart pulsating with fear, and anticipation. "When do we start?"

The Ballad øf Greysøn Ash

SIXTEEN MONTHS AFTER THE WELL

Billy sat on the couch in Greyson's living room, waiting. Ash-Lea sat beside him, sporting her 'puppies are my jam' shirt, depicting a bandana-wearing dog playing a guitar. She yawned. It was a sunny spring-break morning, golden light streaming in through the gigantic windows which lined the back of Greyson's house. The aroma of the breakfast Billy had missed out on still hung in the air, making his tummy rumble.

"Any idea how long this is going to take?" Ash-Lea slouched and plunked her feet up on the coffee table. She slid her phone out of her pocket and started clicking at the screen.

"No idea," Billy said with a yawn. "I know exactly as much as you do about what Greyson is doing." Billy pulled his phone out of his pocket and flipped it open. It wasn't a fancy smart-phone like Ash-Lea's but it had a really cool game of Snake on it.

Greyson had invited Billy and Ash-Lea over that morning because of something really important he *needed* to show them. They'd been sitting there for almost half an hour, listening to Greyson banging around in his room, talking loudly to himself. Finally, Greyson's steps shuffled down the hall, and Billy sat up, excited that the agonizing wait was over.

"You guys ready?" Greyson's voice asked from the direction of the hallway.

"We died ready, Grey." Ash-Lea flopped her phone onto her lap. "We're just a couple of corpses at this point.'

"Okay," Greyson said, his voice full of steely resolve. But Greyson still didn't appear.

Ash-Lea looked at Billy, her expression somewhere between amused and irritated. "Are we supposed to say the magic word?" she asked.

"No," Greyson said. "I . . . I'm coming."

Ash-Lea picked up a pillow and threw it towards the hallway. "Are you coming today?"

"Yes," Greyson said. "Just . . . okay."

Greyson stepped out of the hall, his arms wide to display his . . . *costume*, Billy decided. He wore a low-necked tank top, under a huge faux fur coat with a gigantic puffy collar that went up to his ears. His jeans were weird looking, with a lot of creases sewn into them. His pants were tucked into untied boots. On top of his head, his hair was gelled into a messy nest. But the oddest part of his appearance was the large bandage on his nose.

"Well?" Greyson asked, adjusting his glasses.

Billy cleared his throat. "Those are cool boots." He honestly thought the boots were cool.

Ash-Lea blinked. "Is this an out-of-season April Fool's joke?"

Greyson gave her a flat look in response.

Ash-Lea leaned forward, scrutinizing his ensemble. "Are you getting ready for Halloween?"

"No." Greyson tugged at the collar of his coat proudly. "Seriously, what do you think?"

"I am not sure where to start," Ash-Lea said, her eyes tracing him from hair to boot. "What happened to your nose?"

"Nothing." Greyson waved the question away. "How do I look?"

Billy looked helplessly at Ash-Lea. He had no idea what to say.

"You look like you're trying to be someone else," Ash-Lea said. She added under her breath to Billy, "And not doing a good job."

Greyson beamed. "Thank you."

"What happened to your nose?" Ash-Lea asked again.

Greyson gave a sheepish grin in response. He had obviously put a lot of effort into the getup and didn't seem interested in letting something like a major nose injury distract from it. He seemed so proud of the outfit, too. But it didn't make any sense. It was as un-Greyson-ish as possible.

"Who are you trying to be?" Billy asked.

Greyson tugged the fluffy lapels of the coat. "Macklemore."

Billy glanced at Ash-Lea, hoping for clarification, but she was too busy grimacing. "I don't know what that is," he admitted.

"He's some kind of singer?" Ash-Lea asked.

"Yeah, a rapper," Greyson agreed.

"Why Macklemore?" Billy asked.

Greyson shrugged, his puffy collar bobbing with the motion. "I looked up famous rappers and his name came up first."

Ash-Lea practically bounced out of her seat. "Did you freaking *Bing* it?" She picked up another pillow and tossed it at him. He caught it. "If you want famous white rappers, why didn't you go with Eminem? That's a no-brainer."

Greyson's expression twisted in confusion. "Who?"

Ash-Lea's mouth dropped open, her lips moved, but nothing came out. Finally, she shook her head. "Why are we having this conversation? I'm more confused than when you first walked in."

Greyson threw the pillow back at Ash-Lea. "Two things, so you like my outfit?" He held his arms out and did a half turn.

Billy and Ash-Lea didn't respond. Billy couldn't.

"Second, I wrote a song I want you to hear."

Billy sat up. "You wrote us a song?"

"No." Greyson shook his head, but seemed to regret it. He cupped his nose with both hands and took a deep breath. "It's not for you. But I want to know your opinion."

"Is it as cool as your outfit?" Ash-Lea winked at Greyson.

"I hope so," Greyson said, tugging up the fuzzy sleeves of his coat. He dug into his pocket, pulled out a piece of paper and cleared his throat. "Oh, I almost forgot."

He ran out of the room and returned a moment later with his laptop. Placing it down on the coffee table, he opened it up, pressed a few buttons, and a drum beat accompanied by what could have been electronic trumpets, began emanating from it. Billy suddenly realized what Greyson was about to do, and his face grew very hot.

Don't, Greyson, Billy begged silently. *You can't do it. You don't have the power.*

Ash-Lea sat frozen beside Billy, her eyes bigger than Billy had ever seen them, as she took in the episode unfolding before them.

Greyson stared at his piece of paper, bobbing to the music in a very Greyson way.

"Okay, okay," Greyson said, bracing himself.

And then he started *rapping*. It was a toneless run of words, delivered without the indescribable artistry most rappers have when performing. What it didn't lack, was how *into it* Greyson was.

"It was a sunny day when I saw you walk my way.
And I knew girl that I needed to say 'Hey'
But you're so cool, and you're so fly,
That you could have your choice of any guy.
So I played it cool, when we went to school.
Because I knew someday that you would look my way.
And here I am girl, and I'm saying that 'Hey'
Because you don't have a boyfriend, I would like to apply."

As he rapped, Ash-Lea grabbed the collar of her shirt with both hands and began to slowly pull it up until she was just peering at their friend over her knuckles. Billy stared at him, unable to react to the performance, but inside his heart pounded in agony.

Then Greyson started dancing.

At first, Billy thought Greyson was about to fall over, but he kept moving, his arms jerking around in an attempt to pop-and-lock. Billy's gripped his knees with both hands as he watched the performance, his own face burning. Greyson's eyes were closed as he went through the obviously rehearsed motions, muttering 'one, and two, and three, and-a four' in time to the music. He lifted his arms in the air, and moved them back and forth, then lifted his feet one after the other. Then repeated the moves. It was unlike any dance Billy had ever been subjected to.

Ash-Lea peered at Billy from the collar of her shirt, horror on her face. "What's happening?" she whispered.

"Dancing?" Billy said, unable to tear his eyes from Greyson.

"Okay," Greyson said as he stopped. He puffed, a bead of sweat on his forehead.

"Grey—" Ash-Lea began.

"One and two . . ." Greyson counted, unaware that Ash-Lea was talking. Then he kept on rapping.

> "I knew that Patrick was no good for you.
> But I was waiting for you to get a clue.
> And you're so smart I knew that you would see,
> That the only guy for you is me.
> I was just waiting for you to make the switch.
> I'm going to make you my number one b—"

"GREY." Ash-Lea lunged forward, slamming the laptop closed.

It took Greyson a few seconds to realize the music had stopped. His dancing slowed and his eyes found Ash-Lea.

"Uh," Greyson said. "What do you think?" He looked at Billy. "How was it?"

"Um . . ." Billy replied eloquently.

Greyson's hand trembled as he talked. "It's not totally finished. And I know I need to practice the dancing."

Ash-Lea dropped back on the couch, clutching the laptop to her chest as if she was afraid Greyson might play the music again.

"I've never seen dancing like that," Billy said truthfully.

"Do you think she'll like it?"

"Greyson," Ash-Lea said. "You . . ."

"Yeah?"

"It wasn't good," Ash-Lea said frankly, but kindly.

Thank you for being you, Ashes, Billy thought.

Greyson shook his hands in protest. "I know, I'm working on it. Billy?"

Billy had been punched in the chest by huge demons before; he'd been beaten almost to death on more than one occasion; but somehow, Greyson asking for feedback on his performance hurt more. "Working on it might help."

"No," Ash-Lea said. She looked like this hurt her too, but she was able to talk through it. She scooted forward on the couch and looked up at him, a kind smile beneath pained eyes. "It's not something you can work on. Greyson, it's a bad idea."

"What?" Greyson asked, not seeming to understand.

"I don't think you should rap your feelings to Quinn. I think it's just a bad idea in general."

Greyson shoulders slacked as he looked at Billy. "What about if I don't dance?"

"Ehhhh," Billy said, feeling like he was being asked to push his best friend in front of a train.

Ash-Lea shook her head. "Don't dance. Don't rap. Don't wear that coat."

Greyson pulled the faux fur tight around him. "I can't wear the coat?"

Ash-Lea put the laptop down next to her. "Greyson, maybe you should sit down."

"No." Greyson straightened. "Whatever you have to say, I can take it standing up defensively. I might even fold my arms." He did.

Ash-Lea bit her lip, thinking. "Greyson, ask yourself why you're rapping, and dancing, and wearing the coat."

Greyson tightened his folded arms. "Because Quinn likes rap. And she's a great dancer. And she likes rappers."

"Does she like Macklemore?" she asked.

Greyson stopped holding the coat as closely. "I . . . I don't know."

"Who is her favorite rapper?"

His arms dropped. "I don't know."

Ash-Lea glanced at Billy, as if for reassurance. Billy was so twisted up inside, he could barely think straight. Ash-Lea, on the other hand, was handling this like a seasoned hostage negotiator.

"Does your rap sound anything like what Quinn likes?" she asked.

Greyson looked at the floor. "I don't know," he said, sounding more and more forlorn.

"When was the last time you rapped?"

"I . . . I've been practicing all month," Greyson muttered.

"So why start now?"

"Because Quinn likes rap." He flopped his arms to his side in frustration. "You're supposed to do things girls like to get their attention."

"There is *some* truth to that," Ash-Lea said. "But you're not supposed to act like someone else."

Greyson thrust out a hand to Billy. "Billy, do you agree?"

127

Billy was looking at Greyson's boots as he talked. He wanted to encourage Greyson, tell him to keep practicing, and that probably wasn't the best idea, but he couldn't hurt Greyson's feelings either. "You're not a good rapper. Yet. Maybe you could be."

Greyson shook his fists in frustration. "She just broke up with Patrick, and I can't risk them getting back together," he said loudly. "This is my chance. I've always liked her. She's always been so, so, so cool. She's next level, man. And it took me a long time to find a Macklemore coat."

"Is that real fur?" Ash-Lea asked.

"Yeah, it's demonhound," Greyson spat back. "No, it's not real."

"Just checking." Ash-Lea smirked and sat back.

Greyson scrunched up his lyrics and stuffed the paper into his pocket. "Well, what am I supposed to do to get her attention?

"You could just tell her," Billy said, and immediately thought the better of it. Ash-Lea had told Billy she loved him more than a year ago and it didn't go over well. It didn't go over badly either. They hadn't talked about it since. She'd probably changed her mind by now, which would suck, because a girl like Ash-Lea liking him was a dream come true. But Ash-Lea deserved better than chubby, dorky, demonically-bad-trouble-attracting him. He couldn't date her. She had to know it was a bad idea.

Greyson missed the opportunity to illuminate Billy's hypocrisy. "You don't just tell a girl like Quinn that you like her. She's special. She's beautiful, and smart, and scary tough."

"Why don't you tell her that?" Ash-Lea said.

Greyson looked at her with an open mouth. "I . . . I couldn't. She's special."

"She won't know if you don't say anything," Billy said. Though, he wasn't sure that was true. Greyson had carried a freaking huge torch for Quinn for a good three years now. It was pretty obvious how he felt.

"Rapping isn't your thing," Ash-Lea said. "Stick with what you're good at, like computers."

"Oh yeah," Greyson said dryly. "I'll go email her. That'll knock her socks off."

Ash-Lea laughed. "Nah, do something that's you. Like make all the street lights flash 'I love you' in Morse Code."

Greyson paused. "That's not a terrible idea at all. She knows Morse Code. But she might not know it's for her. It would have to be 'I love you, Quinn'."

"How about something that doesn't put people in danger," Billy suggested.

"Right. Good point, too." Greyson clicked his fingers rapidly. "Like I could make her TV flash. Or it doesn't even have to be Morse code. I could get the Fidgets to . . . to do something." Greyson's excitement faded. "But she doesn't care about that stuff. I know what she likes, but my Fidgets aren't cool enough. She's seen them. And she's seen all the stuff I can do on computers. I need to do something new. Like wire a million dollars into her bank account."

Billy's jaw hit the floor. *Uh, hello?* "You can do that?" Billy asked.

"I don't think breaking the law is a great idea either." Ash-lea picked up the pillow and back-handed Billy with it. "And she doesn't need money. Her house is five times bigger than yours. And in case you forgot, yours is gigantic."

"There has to be something. Something I can do. Something . . . meaningful."

Greyson strode around the coffee table to retrieve his laptop, and Ash-Lea snatched it up instinctively. Greyson tugged on it as if she'd picked it up to hand it to him. "Uh, Ashes? Can I have that?"

With a miserable look at Billy, she let the laptop go.

"I just need to keep practicing. That's all," Greyson said. "I'm at least as good as Macklemore."

129

Ash-Lea bobbed her head and pointed at Greyson. "While that is probably true, I wouldn't be your friend if I couldn't tell you that this is not a good idea."

Greyson slipped his laptop into what must have been a gigantic pocket in the coat. "I'll show you. This is going to blow her away. You'll see."

"How can you blow her away when you can't even blow your nose?" Ash-Lea asked.

Greyson froze, scowling at Ash-Lea.

"How did you break your nose?" Billy asked.

Greyson's grumpy demeanor faded and he glanced at Billy. Greyson seemed to shrink six inches before his eyes.

"I . . ." Greyson said, tugging on his puffy sleeves.

"Yeah?" Ash-Lea asked.

"I was da. . ." he muttered the rest.

"Sorry, didn't catch that," Ash-Lea said.

"I was . . . dabbing."

Ash-Lea snorted and she stomped the ground with her feet. She looked like she was getting ready to pop. She snatched up a couch pillow and buried her face in it, letting out muffled laughter as her body shook.

Billy felt the laughter rising, his lips twitching as he watched Ash-Lea lose it. Then he saw the agonized look in Greyson's eyes. He didn't feel like laughing after that.

"Are you okay?" Billy asked.

Greyson looked at his really cool boots. "I feel pretty stupid. And it hurts."

Billy put a hand on Ash-Lea's shoulder and nudged her. She lifted her head, sighing, then she took in Greyson's expression and the laughter faded.

"I'm sorry, Grey. That looks like it hurts. You broke your nose—" her lip trembled, but she kept it under control, "—dabbing?"

"Yeah." Greyson pulled up the giant collar over his head. "It was part of the choreography."

Billy and Ash-Lea sat there watching Greyson as he stood in the middle of the room with his head covered for a good thirty seconds. Finally, he walked over to the couch and plopped down in the middle of his best friends. He poked his head out of the coat like a turtle peeking out of his shell.

"I'm not being myself. Am I?"

Billy patted Greyson's leg. "Not really."

Ash-Lea punched Greyson's other leg. "Let me tell you from personal experience that if you can't impress a girl just by being yourself, then she's not worth it. You go out of your way to knock her socks off, and you're setting a precedent that you can't maintain."

"Yeah." He pulled the paper out of his pocked at stared at it. "What if she actually likes my rapping and wants me to write another one? It took me about four hours to write that."

"Really?" Ash-Lea sucked in a breath and blew it out. "Wow. That is . . . not something I think you need to do again. Ever."

"Ashes," Greyson said, sounding hurt.

"No, I mean." Ash-Lea grumbled. "It's just a lot of work doing something you don't do, just for a girl."

"The girls who are worth it are worth putting in some effort," Greyson said.

"Of course they are," Ash-Lea replied. "But within the context of who you already are."

"I . . . I guess." Greyson sunk back into the couch.

"There is no doubt that Quinn is really, really cool. But I don't know anyone worth breaking your nose dabbing over." Ash-Lea snorted, then quickly reigned in the laugher.

Greyson looked up at the ceiling. "Do you guys want to hear the last verse?"

Ash-Lea scrunched up her face. "Nah."

Greyson rolled his head in Billy's direction. "Billy, what do you think?"

"About hearing the last verse?"

"About all of this."

Billy squeezed Greyson's knee. "I think you're the smartest person I know. You're very cool. And very nerdy. And that's a winning combo. Either Quinn will see it, or she won't. And if she doesn't, she doesn't deserve you."

"Thanks, man." Greyson scrumpled up the rap lyrics and tossed it across the room in the general direction of the kitchen. "I'm going to ask her out—without rapping it."

"She's lucky to have a guy like you fancy her," Ash-Lea squeezed Greyson's other knee.

"Heh," Greyson replied, pulling at the fur on the front of his coat. "She's a gorgeous cheerleader. A *college* cheerleader. You couldn't throw a stone at school without hitting someone who doesn't have a crush on her."

Billy tried to figure out what Greyson had just said, but gave up and just nodded in agreement.

"Why don't you go over there right now and ask?" Billy suggested.

"I was thinking of waiting until my nose healed."

"How long with that be?" Ash-Lea asked.

"Five to seven weeks."

Ash-Lea leaned forward, a smirk on her face. "You're a paragon of courage, Grey."

"I am who I am," he said with a smile. "No reason to do anything unnatural on account of a girl."

A Swarm of Wasps

Alec sat in the corner of the human building, waiting as the other spiders spun webs, preparing to sleep for the day. The soldiers worked in quiet exhaustion, wearily binding their string against the tin walls. He clicked his claws on the concrete under him in a prayer to their god, Mengodordum. Alec observed as best he could through failing eyes. He wasn't old, too young to have his eyesight fading as it was—though he wasn't completely blind yet. He'd hoped forming a coil in the earth realm would help him reclaim his sight, but it did not. Near blindness was simply a part of him now, no matter which plane he walked.

He did not need to see the spiders around him clearly to know they were all tired and scared. On a day as cold as this, the fires of Hidden Corner would be lit and the spiders would sleep in warmth. But there was no warmth to be had here. They could not risk arousing the suspicion of any more humans, especially by lighting fires in a disused structure such as this.

Alec scented his friend approach and turned to see the familiar outline of Aegeus limping forward.

"How do you fare?" Alec asked.

Aegeus gave a dry laugh. "Not good, my friend. That human stung me well." He pressed his leg against his side where the bullet had penetrated. The previous day, they had been hiding in a shed which housed cattle. The cattle were not fond of the presence of spiders and it was not long before the ruckus aroused the attention of the cowherd. The human had brought his gun with him and managed to shoot Aegeus before they had a chance to flee.

"We will find something and bind you right soon," Alec said.

"I certainly hope so," Aegeus replied, a smile in his tone. "I do not wish for my discarded form to remain in this realm until reality implodes."

Alec knew that Aegeus was scared. The wound was unfamiliar, and much more painful than he would admit. They were all soldiers, and understood injuries from arrows and swords. But human bullets were still mysterious. If the armies of Aberdem wished success in taking the human planet and those beyond, Alec thought they had best learn about firearms quickly. But nobody was listening to the opinion of blind leg soldiers.

"Let me see that injury," Yadira, the healer of the group, said. She was an older spider, probably past the age of retirement. But many spiders had enthusiastically entered the Human Realm in hopes of witnessing the victory of General Krios over the Demonseed. Though that battle had not resulted in the victory they had expected.

Yadira was not a healer in truth. She had worked with many, and seen many more years of battle than any spider here. But she was not trained. She was simply helping the best she could in a desperate situation.

"You bleed too much," Yadira said. "As your superior officer, I command you to stop."

"Yes, second lieutenant," Aegeus agreed, a grin in a voice laced with pain.

Yadira ran her claws over Aegeus fur, inspecting the wound. "I'll need to shave around the penetration for the web to bind it shut properly. But I'm worried it's like an arrow head that has broken off inside you. It needs to be removed. There are tools in this realm to perform such an operation, but none fit for a spider's claws."

"We need to get back home," Alec said.

Yadira made a noncommittal sound. "Somedemon would have to open a portal for us on this side. Nobody is coming to rescue us with the Threshold burned."

"How badly is it damaged?" Aegeus asked.

"You'd have to ask our intrepid leader," Yadira said, and not kindly.

Somehow sensing that the conversation was about her, the leader of their group, Hedda, started over.

"How is Aegeus doing?" Hedda asked Yadira, assumed authority in her tone.

Alec thought it funny that she would ask Yadira instead of Aegeus himself, but he was not in a position to question her. Though only a lieutenant, Hedda was the senior ranking officer and they were soldiers lost on enemy soil, in need of leadership. Moreover, she was a Balchen, by far the largest spider in their luckless group—and if spiders listened to anyone, it was the biggest spider in the room. She wasn't well respected amongst the stranded group, but that wasn't a requirement to lead. There wasn't a single one among them who was not afraid.

"Aegeus is in need of a fully equipped spider physician," Yadira explained. "The bullet...the human arrow head is still inside. The bleeding will not stop."

"Will he survive tonight?" Hedda asked.

Yadira poked at Aegeus's wound. "I can stop it up enough with what I have, but I do not recommend waiting beyond tomorrow."

"Let's get a few hours rest," Hedda said. "We'll do what we can before the sun ceases burning."

"What's for supper?" Aegeus asked. "I'm famished."

"We acquired some dogs," Yadira said.

"Dog again?" Aegeus complained. "I grow tired of dog. What I wouldn't give for a nice, fat human."

"We cannot risk drawing attention to ourselves," Hedda said. "Especially without a means to escape. We're lucky that cowherd did not have all his guns on him. It's known that humans have at least six or seven guns on them. Even the children. This realm is not a safe place."

"Understood, ma'am," Aegeus said.

Alec saw Aegeus look in his direction. Though he couldn't make out his friend's face very well, he got the impression he was rolling his eyes.

"Those human Wasps have our trail," Hedda said, considering the room about them.

Alec shivered at the name. The band of humans that had been pursuing them for two turns were relentless, a kind of madness unique to humans driving them. They wore heavy coats depicting a frenzied-looking wasp on the back. So far, they had evaded the humans, but it was only a matter of time before the Wasps closed in. The battle between the Wasps and the spiders was sure to be a brutal one.

"Alec," Hedda ordered, "I want you to help with preparations to welcome them should they find us this day."

"How so?"

"Get up off your spinner and find out." She grabbed Alec by the chin and pointed his head towards the far wall. "There is a stack of weighty metal tubes over there, they can be used as a trap. Go help the spiders working on that. And that human vehicle in the middle of the floor is heavy. String it up against the roof near the anterior door so it may crush them when they enter."

136

"Yes, lieutenant," Alec said. He knew the vehicle she meant, he'd almost walked straight into it when they'd arrived.

Despite his eyes, Alec felt more energetic than the other spiders here. Possibly because he was not able to fight and hunt like the rest of them and had been left out of much of the action. His impairment was a frustration for him and his fellow spiders.

Alec found the pipes Hedda spoke of, three other spiders were already at work raising the poles and sticking them to the wall. Alec picked one up, the attempt taking more effort than expected as he hefted it off the floor. They seemed to be forged of some kind of iron—he was no blacksmith. The Human Realm was fascinating, Alec mused. They had many things that the Demonic Realm simply did not. A few hundred years ago, humans stole the knowledge of how to manipulate lightning from the demons, and that had led to many things such as automobiles and blenders. The wisest of demons had attempted to bring the inventions back to the Demonic Realm, but the atmosphere there was not conducive to maintaining machines that were not powered by steam. They corroded quickly, their parts falling to pieces. There was an Eiteeguy residing by the White Spire who had managed to run electronics in the Demonic Realm for extended periods of time. Alec would like to ask him how, someday, if fate would allow it.

Alec stuck a glob of string to the pipes and then attached the pipes to the wall. The humans were a clever species, he thought as he worked. They didn't like being surprised by demons, but they weren't out to kill them, not in the same way demons sought to kill humans. Over the years, humans had forgotten the reality of who demons were, and they made up stories about their genesis. Most human no longer believed demons truly existed.

Demons, on the other hand, were determined to eradicate humans. But there were so few humans, and without their guns they were helpless. If every demon were to enter Earth they would cover the surface fifty times over. Humans didn't understand that. They weren't prepared for it. And moreover, they weren't trying to stop the demons. Alec simply couldn't see them as a threat like the Winged King said they were. It felt more like the words of Demon Gods that wanted an increase of power, and not an actual requisite to preserving the demon way of life.

When they had finished attaching the pipes along the wall, Alec lay a thick cord of spider string across them. Meanwhile, his fellow spiders set a trip string on the floor, parallel to the wall. Alec allowed the spiders with better eye sight to connect the two strings to complete the trap, so if any human walked too close all the pipes would tumble onto them, cracking them across their soft heads. Once finished, he listened to his comrades congratulating each other on their work.

"Have a good rest, Alec," one of the spiders, Calla, said. "Perhaps you are not such a burden as I had supposed."

"It is my purpose to give you a standard to which you can aspire," Alec replied.

They laughed as they scuttled off towards their webs.

"Oh, Calla, we have to hang the forked vehicle," he called. Nobody responded. He could hear spiders all around him, the walls rattling in the wind. They had likely not heard him, and he did not wish to rush about shouting their name and sounding the fool. *Fine, I'll do it myself. In truth, I am no burden.*

Alec found the forked vehicle easily enough. It was an odd-looking thing, with a prong much like a fork on the front. Alec had not seen one before. Its design was curious. *Perhaps the humans used these for jousting, or some other sport.* He climbed up the wall and along the ceiling until he was directly above the forked vehicle and dropped a rope. He secured the machine and began to raise it. The thin metal of the roof above him groaned at the weight and he felt his claw cutting through.

"Hold," Yadira said, appearing beside him. She extended her own rope and gripped the forked vehicle and assisted him with raising it to the ceiling. "Grip the girders, they are far sturdier than the tin of the roof."

Alec felt with his claws and found the girders she spoke of. "Many thanks."

"I'm doing this for myself," Yadira chuckled. "Tearing the roof down upon us is something I wish to avoid. It is too cold this day."

"How fares Aegeus?" Alec asked.

Yadira sighed. "He sleeps. He is weaker than he lets on. The bleeding has stopped for now, but we must remove the bullet as soon as we are able. A few hours rest will do him good, but too many will not."

"Thank you for helping my friend."

"You are an odd spider," Yadira observed. She held the forked vehicle in place as Alec strung it up against the girders.

"Why do you say that?" Alec asked.

"Thanking me for assisting another. It's more a human trait than a demon."

"I hear my great, great, great grandmother was a human."

Yadira chuckled. "I would not be surprised."

"Nonetheless, I am grateful for you assisting my friend. He's been my eyes when things were particularly dark."

"You do well for a blind spider."

"I can see many things if I hold it close to my eyes and squint. It allows me to stumble through. And I can make out most large objects, especially if the light is good."

"Alec," Yadira said, suddenly close to his ear, her voice a whisper. Her tone made Alec freeze. "It would not do to antagonize the humans. As things stand, they outnumber us seven billion to twenty."

Alec shivered at the intensity in her words. "I know," he whispered in turn. "If we kill them here, others will hunt for us."

"A fact to keep in mind when those Wasps begin to swarm." Yadira scurried away.

The Wasps had been relentless in their pursuit. Once every seven days for the last two turns they appeared. The spiders had managed to escape each time, but the Wasps grew more cunning with each attempt. It had been seven days since they had seen them last and there was little doubt that they would appear this evening. Alec longed for the running and hiding to end. He wished he could flee into the wilderness, but the snow, which painted the tops of the mountains, would kill them as sure as human bullets.

"How goes the work?" Hedda called, rousing Alec from his thoughts.

"It goes well, lieutenant," Alec replied as he returned to his work.

The next task was to install the pull rope that would break the strings binding the forked vehicle to the ceiling. There would be little chance a human standing underneath would notice it coming for them. He climbed down the wall and rigged a thin rope between the floor and the wall so a human passing underneath would sever the rope unintentionally. It was a good trap.

"Ho, Alec," Hedda called.

Her voice came from the front of the building, though he couldn't see her. He scurried in what he hoped was her direction.

"Over here, gravelmole," Hedda called from somewhere to his left.

He turned and walked through a narrow doorway. Hedda stood in the small room at the front of the building. Windows let in dusky light, covered by some kind of curtain. There was a table by the far wall. Other than that, Alec could not make out any more interesting features.

"See these?" she asked, indicating something that looked like closets. Alec nodded. Hedda opened the door. "I have hidden spring traps inside. We'll place some string across this room. The humans are sure to pass through here. Once they hit the traps, they will be shot through with this glass."

"Brilliant," Alec said. "That will surely stop them in their tracks."

Hedda nodded. "It will kill them and end one of our woes."

"True. Though I worry we captured the attention of that human who shot Aegeus."

Hedda ground her mandibles. "We did. I am hoping he is too scared to pursue us. But there are so many damned humans in their realm. It will not take long for them to find us if they band together." She raked a claw across her head. "These preparations will do for this morning. We all need some sleep and we must get moving before Aegeus loses too much blood. Confounding our troubles are the Wasps who are due this evening."

Hedda was unpleasant company, though she did take responsibility for the groups' safety seriously.

Somespider had recovered a collection of heavy blankets. They were thick and not particularly warm. They seemed too large and rigid for a human to sleep under, but he could not imagine what else they would be. Alec did not mind, he was happy to not sleep on the cold cement, or on a web strung to the metal walls as they shook in the icy breeze. He dragged one over next to Aegeus and set it down. He lifted his head, saw Alec settling in beside him, and went back to sleep.

Before the earth sun had disappeared from the sky, Hedda's voice echoed through the building. "Up, you slack sacks. We must move," she called.

Alec had not even realized he'd fallen to sleep.

"So early?" Aegeus yawned.

"You're the one bleeding to death in this accursed realm," Hedda snarled. "You tell me if you wish to die here or not."

Alec turned to Aegeus. "How do you fare?"

"Ah, not too terribly," Aegeus grunted. "The bleeding has slowed. The pain has not."

"Can you move?" Hedda asked, much closer.

"I can," Aegeus replied. "The sleep did some good. Though I am not fit for a fight if it comes to it."

"You'd best stop antagonizing me, then," Hedda laughed. No one else did. "I scouted last day and found a building only a few hundred legs away. It appears to contain utensils we can use for the operation."

"That sounds . . . better than nothing," Aegeus said. "Let's go."

Aegeus moaned in pain as he stood. Alec extended a leg and helped his friend to his claws.

Aegeus chuckled to himself. "The blind spider helping me? I will not live this down."

"I sincerely hope you have the opportunity to not live this down."

Aegeus patted Alec on the shoulder. "Let us see what this night brings."

"What language do they speak in these parts?" Hedda called to the room.

"I believe they have two human dialects," Alec replied. "Predominantly, English and Spanish."

"Do you know them?"

"Some. I was making a study of human languages before my eyes failed."

Alec could feel Hedda's eye on him. "How did a blind spider make it into Krios' ranks?" she asked, her voice hard.

"I . . . lied to get here. I hoped crossing the Threshold would restore my sight. It did not."

"Well, a hindrance you've been so far, perhaps you can make use of yourself. You'll stay here waiting for the humans, should they come."

"Yes, ma'am," Alec said, fear creeping into his thorax.

"Wait until midnight. If they have not appeared then follow us," Hedda ordered.

"Yes, lieutenant." Alec did not know how a blind spider was to follow his company, assuming he survived the swarming Wasps; it was likely Hedda never expected him to. He was a burden to all around him, and demons had no tolerance for useless spiders. But that was a fly he would bind once it was in his web.

Hedda disappeared into the fog beyond Alec's vision and he felt Aegeus pat him reassuringly on the arm.

"What am I to do?" Alec asked.

"Crush them with the forked vehicle. Should that fail, use your words. Humans have forgotten demons, they are afraid of us. Threaten them with colorful words."

"But they have guns, and they speak clearly enough with those. And faster than I could utter," Alec moaned.

"You'll be fine," Aegeus replied. "It's unlikely the Wasps will follow us here. Just rest and have sweet dreams of the agony our surgeon will wreak on me removing this bullet."

Alec snickered. "You stay brave yourself. That spider will save your life."

"Or end it. We shall see."

A grinding noise echoed through the warehouse as a door was lifted at the far end of the building.

"Come, the sky is darkening. Time to move," Hedda called.

Spiders began shuffling through the building, no more than grey smudges in Alec' eyes. He felt empty as Aegeus followed, limping. A shadowlurk waited at the door and may have looked back at Alec before disappearing underneath. But if they did, he couldn't truly tell.

Alec settled back onto his blanket. There was nothing more to do but wait, staring at the fogged world around him. He stood and gathered up all the blankets he could find and stacked them on top of one another. The result was a fairly comfortable pillow. For the next two hours, Alec drifted in and out of sleep, occasionally jolting awake as he remembered where he was. The night began to grow darker, he decided he'd best stay alert.

Alec climbed onto the ceiling and started exploring the walls. On one wall, he found a small window positioned close to the ceiling. He hung next to it, peering outside through squinted eyes. The night was dark, the trees dancing in the wind, causing the unnaturally bright human lights to cast shadows that jittered across the walls. He wished he could see. The others talked about the buildings and the sights of the Human Realm with awe. The sunlight was incredible. He had never beheld such light in all his life, but still it was a blur. He wished he could see the vehicles as they raced on the hard asphalt, creating their ghastly aromas, or more than the outline of towering buildings formed of cement and glass. Instead, he saw the ground, leaves, and refuse blowing in the wind, and little more.

Alec could simply wait up in the loft, he decided. Let the humans come if they did, and let them trip the traps if they were so unfortunate. But any deaths here would attract the attention of more humans, and they would certainly look into the circumstances surrounding any deaths. A forked vehicle did not often fall from the ceiling, he imagined. If humans died here, then more would come searching for them. And there was no way for Alec and his fellow spiders to escape from the realm. Not unless somedemon came for them. Each day they spent on the Earth, rescue seemed more unlikely.

Alec started in surprise as voices came from outside the window. He paused, listening. He couldn't tell if the movement in the yard below were humans or the play of shadows. He waited.

"Nobody is climbing on me," a distinct voice said.

Alec scuttled back. He knew that voice. She was a Wasp. The biggest one they had. Bigger than he, with thick, muscular arms. The Wasps had tracked them down—they'd never failed to before. He felt his heart drumming in his thorax. They were here. He didn't know how many there were, but he was alone against them all. And he couldn't see.

He tapped his claws against the roof. *Mengodordum,* he prayed. *What do I do?*

He waited, listening to their indistinct voices outside the window. They were moving things around in the yard, stacking them against the wall. He couldn't fathom what they were planning to do, the window was too small for a human to fit through.

A shadow fell over the window and Alec cringed close to the ceiling. The Wasps were peering inside. Scouting for spiders, perhaps. He had to do something, something to scare them away so they would not enter the building. But he had nothing, no weapons, no way to see.

A mad idea filled him and Alec rushed forward, scampering across the ceiling. He slammed into the wall by the window and the Wasps outside screamed in surprise. They tumbled backwards onto the ground, belting out a chorus of pain. They scampered away into the darkness and Alec let out a long breath.

I've scared the swarm away, he thought, smiling. They had no way to know how many spiders waited for them inside. He walked back to the blankets in the loft, his heart still drumming, and lay down. It hadn't been too long since the other spiders departed. Perhaps their scent was still strong enough to follow, if the breeze hadn't blown it away.

Alec knew he didn't have time to linger. Rising on his trembling legs, he walked across the ceiling and down the back wall to the door when he heard a distant bang echo across the building.

They're coming in anyway, he realized. *Those humans are insane. Or brave. The spring-loaded glass,* Alec remembered.

He clambered across the dark warehouse floor, racing the Wasps to reach the front of the building. His claw caught on a blanket and his legs shot out from under him. Tumbling over, he dug his claw into the concrete, stopping the roll, and he slid into the wall with an echoing thud. The light in the warehouse had diminished greatly since the sun had disappeared and the room was too dark to see anything with his half-blind eyes. He fumbled at the wall, searching for the tripwire when suddenly the wall disappeared and he stumbled forward into the entry room.

He was inside the entryway, beside the glass trap, somehow not tripping the string as he entered. He prayed he would not trip it as he exited.

Voices could be heard outside, arguing in their human tongue, and Alec backed up. He felt an unfamiliar spider string brush his leg and he froze. Carefully, he leaned backwards, leaving his leg in place as he twisted his body out of the way. Slowly maneuvering through the doorway, Alec had one claw on the floor beyond when he slipped. He hit the ground, his leg tugging on the string. The trap sprung, throwing glass into the room with explosive force. It whizzed past his face, spraying his cheek with shards. The room filled with the shrill sound of breaking glass, the pieces flying into the roof, and scraping across the floor.

"What the hell was that?" a voice shouted from beyond the door.

The front door opened and Alec jumped, clambering up to the ceiling inside the warehouse. He tucked himself into the corner and squinting, watched as six figures passed into the room below him. The Wasps whispered to one another. Alec wondered if they had especially good eyesight for humans, because he couldn't make out the light from any torches.

The door below Alec slammed shut. He wasn't sure what had done it, the wind, or perhaps Hedda had set that up as a distraction for when the vehicle fell.

The forked vehicle, he remembered.

Alec drew some string and flung it out at the machine just as it fell from the ceiling directly towards the humans on the ground beneath it. His string caught and he pulled, clenching his mouth closed to hide the sound of effort.

The forked vehicle descent curved slightly, smashing into the warehouse floor with a boom behind the humans. He heard the humans shouting, stumbling towards the wall of pipes.

Oh no, Alec whispered.

One of the humans must have tripped the string as the pipes popped off the wall and began clattering to the floor.

The humans screamed in surprise. Then they screamed in pain.

The pipes seemed to fall for an eternity, and all Alec could do was hang in the darkness, listening to them wailing. If any of them died, it would be the end of all the spiders in the realm.

The one human that seemed unaffected by the chaos ran over to the pipes and started throwing them off the other Wasps.

"You okay?" it asked.

They began talking, too quietly for Alec to hear. One of the Wasps wasn't moving.

Oh, no. Alec thought once more.

The Wasp dragged the unmoving one behind the forked vehicle, as if it was some protection against a demon who could drop from the ceiling on to them. Another human pulled herself from under the pipes, cussing in English as she did.

Amazingly, it seemed like the traps had incapacitated all but two of the Wasps. They huddled close to the vehicle, whispering to one another. The two remained standing, holding heavy-looking clubs in their hands. If he didn't stop them, they would pursue him when he tried to escape. There was no way he could leave while two still had fight in them. He remained still in the shadows, unsure of his next move. Then one stepped away from the forked vehicle, just far enough that he could reach the Wasp if he tried.

He attached a string to the ceiling and let himself drop, swinging down towards the Wasp. He slammed into the human and wrapped his legs around her. She screamed as he picked her up and tossed her away, careful not to throw her harder than necessary. Alec slammed into the wall, which appeared from the darkness before he expected it. Excitement and fear mingled in his blood and he forgot how to hold onto the vertical surface. He started stumbling backwards.

"Don't even think about it," the other Wasp shouted.

Alec froze at the sound, looking for the Wasp amongst the shadows. The human ran at him. Alec heard it more than saw it, imagining the weapon in the Wasp's hand was a sword. He let his arm flail out, hoping to stop the Wasp from stinging him. His leg met nothing but air.

Then the Wasp crashed into him, knocking the air from his lungs. The human bounced off and landed on the pipes with a clattering rattle. Alec hissed in pain and scampered off, stumbling over the pipes and up the back wall of the warehouse.

The Wasps buzzed back and forth, and a light suddenly appeared, illuminating the whole building. It barely made things clearer for Alec. It only took them a moment to shine the light on him. He stood up, striving to stop his shaking legs from being too apparent. But he held his leg up defensively. He was simply too scared to control himself.

"How many are you?" the Wasp with the light shouted.

Alec planted his claws. "Please leave me alone," he said in his native language, hoping the unfamiliar words would be enough to scare them. They didn't react like scared humans should. They stayed where they were.

I need to leave, he thought. *I can't take much more of this. Maybe I can knock them over and make a break for it.*

Alec jumped off the wall and rushed them, charging at the Wasp standing in the open. At the last moment the Wasp moved impossibly fast, and Alec realized he wasn't running at a human, but at a shadow cast by the torch in the human's hand. He didn't know what to do, so he kept running.

Oh Mengodordum, Alec thought. *You're making a fool of yourself.*

That's when his legs hit the pipes on the ground and he stumbled to his side. He could hear the Wasp with the torch screaming wildly beside him, but he was simply trying to not fall onto his back. He tumbled sideways and found his leg meeting something solid. The human screamed as his claw dug into her stomach and then stopped. Hot pain shot up to his shoulder as his claw ripped free.

I've killed her, Alec thought. *Oh, Mengodordum.*

"No," the Wasp behind him cried.

Alec turned in a slow circle, limping on his leg with the missing claw. The pain caused tears to form in his eyes and run down his cheeks. "Human," Alec said in his most threatening voice, his eyes on the man's shadow.

"Chris," the Wasp behind Alec shouted.

Alec flinched at the noise. She didn't seem like someone dying, just angry.

A clanging sound came from the forked vehicle as Chris the Human struck it with his weapon and Alec cringed again. If Chris could see better than he, than Alec was making a fool of himself, indeed. He was out numbered and out skilled. There was little he could do against them all. He needed to get out of here, now. With the Wasp behind him down, there was only Chris left. He just needed to shove him over and escape.

Alec lunged forward, his legs outstretched, trying to topple Chris, but ended up slamming into the forked vehicle. He'd mistaken part of the machine for the human. He pulled back, but his claw was stuck in some kind of cloth attached to the vehicle. Panic exploded inside him as he drew back; his claw would not come free.

Chris the Human did not miss the opportunity. He swept his weapon down, slamming on to Alec's limb. Alec gasped in agony as his leg became lodged between the forked vehicle and Chris' weapon. The human pushed down, crying out in effort. Alec's restraint left him and he started to flail, struggling to pull free from the vice. His claws slipped on the cement, the vehicle screeching as it was dragged an inch across the floor.

"Chris?" the Wasp called again. Wherever she was, she wasn't coming to help. At least he'd accomplished that much. "Chris, you okay?"

Chris grunted as he crushed the weapon down on Alec's leg, but he didn't seem to have any other plans. Chris could attack without loosing Alec's leg. The human had no way to know Alec couldn't see him clearly, that he couldn't see anything clearly. He was trapped and surrounded and blind, his missing claw throbbed in agony. He stopped struggling, his legs failing him, and he collapsed to the ground. Without bidding, a whining sound escaped Alec's throat before he could stop it. Tears welled in his eyes and he sniffled, wiping them away with his free foreleg. He was an utter failure; unfit to fight in Krios' armies, and unable to keep his comrades trapped in the Human Realm safe.

"What the hell?" Chris asked.

Alec winced at the sound. He could feel his body trembling like a hatchling's. He'd never been so humiliated.

"Are you . . . crying?" Chris asked.

"No," Alec insisted as he sniffled again.

Chris made a sound like a nervous human laugh. "You're as scared as I am."

It's scared? Alec thought. *These are the Wasps that have been swarming after us for turns. How could any of them be afraid?* "I just want to go home," he confessed.

"Chris," the Wasp called from across the warehouse. "You'd better answer me."

"I'm okay," Chris shouted in response. "You okay?"

"I'm bleeding, but it's not bad. Kind of hard to stand right now, though. Where is it?"

Alec followed the silhouette of the bat to where Chris stood, almost invisible against the shadowed background. Chris stared down at him, an outline of a man in the darkness, like from the stories they had been told as hatchlings. Alec knew that this was the end. This Wasp would not let him see the sun rise again.

"I'm not sure where it is," Chris called back. "How many of you are there?" he whispered to Alec.

"We number nineteen and one, sir," Alec replied.

"I, uh. I guess I'm supposed to kill you now," Chris said, his voice unsure.

Alec closed his blind eyes and bowed his head. "I understand."

"Give me a good reason not to."

Alec raised his head, confused. He had not expected that. "I just saved your life."

"What are you talking about?"

"This forked vehicle would have crushed you, but I pulled it out of the way."

"But you guys put it on the roof in the first place."

"I was following orders to place it there. Nobody ordered me to not kill you with it. And the glass in the entry way would have skewered you, had I not sprung the trap early."

"You set off the glass trap by door so it wouldn't hurt us?"

"I did."

Chris scoffed in doubt. "I wouldn't believe you, but . . . you're crying."

Alec's lip trembled. "I just want to go home."

"Are you killing humans?" Chris insisted.

Alec shook his head vigorously. "We have not dared. We have been feeding on dogs and cats. I have told Hedda if she continues to steal pets, we will be discovered before we can find a way home."

Chris lessened the pressure on Alec's leg, just slightly. "Hedda's your leader?"

"Assumed leader. Yes."

"Tell him—"

"Her."

"Tell her she'd better stop killing animals. We're on to you."

Alec felt a rush of fear. A confrontation would end in bloodshed. And the remaining spiders would be hunted mercilessly. "Please, don't. You will come for your deaths. Hedda has no love for humans. We are simply trying to survive as we seek a way to return home."

"If she keeps killing," Chris said, his voice dangerous, "she's the one who has invited death to your door. Get out of here and tell them, before we finish you off, too."

Chris pulled the bat backwards, and Alec's leg dropped. It tingled painfully. He pulled it close to his thorax and massaged his shoulder.

"Get out of here, okay?" Chris said. "Just go."

Alec took an uncertain step backwards. "Are you sincere, human?" he whispered.

"You did try to kill us." Chris' voice was full of doubt. "Just get out before I change my mind."

Alec nodded. The human wanted to fight as little as he did. "I . . . I will remember your name," he said. An ally in a human, even a Wasp, was better than an enemy.

"What's yours?" Chris whispered.

"My name? 'Tis Alec," he said, bobbing his head in greeting out of sheer habit. "Thank you for my life, Chris."

Alec turned on shaking legs, limping, and scampered across the warehouse. He found the door at the far end, a long shaft of light sneaking under it. He lifted it and spied the outline of Chris the Human next to the remains of the forked vehicle. Alec nodded in thanks. By Mengodordum's might, he should not have survived that encounter. Alec slipped into the chilly night, letting the door slam closed behind him.

Gløssary

Aegeus: Demon. Male. Tremanchen. Leg soldier in the Spider Horde. Friend of Alec. Currently stranded in the Human Realm.

Alec: Demon. Male. Tremanchen. Knows several human languages, but lost his eyesight at a young age. Currently stranded in the Human Realm.

Auburn Fawn: Human. Female. Five feet, nine inches tall. Highly athletic and skilled at baseball, her most striking physical feature is her curly red hair. Exceptionally fast and known for her astute observations about her opposition. Member of the Sugar House Wasps.

Balchen: Second largest of the race of spiders. Approximately 12-15 feet tall.

Belle Thacker: Human. Female. Nineteen years old. She has a muscular physique with many tattoos. Favors a shaved head. Formally attended Bleakwood High. Highly advanced at explosives manufacturing, though lacks training.

Beryl Azure: Human. Female. Six feet, four inches tall. Commonly called Bee, or Arms, on account of her exceptionally muscular forearms. Member of the Sugar House Wasps.

Bulfeghow: Demonic beasts of burden which can grow between fifteen and thirty feet tall. Often used as mounts by the larger races.

Calla: Demon. Female. Tremanchen. Leg soldier in the Spider Horde. Currently stranded in the Human Realm.

Corthas: The apprentice primarily responsible for the forging of the Warrior's Triune. Son of Melferim and a human. Nephew of the Patriarch.

Crystal Glass. Human. Female. Six foot, one inch tall. Has round cheeks and short blonde hair. Is usually quiet and timid, but is a passionate and skilled baseball player. Expert at lock picking, and thievery. Member of the Sugar House Wasps.

Ember Ascua: Human. Female. Five feet, eleven inches tall. Dark wavy hair, deep copper skin. Captain of the Sugar House Wasp minor league baseball team.

Fildoran: A dragon-like demon, often mistaken for the mythological Japanese dragon. Can be anywhere from thirty to two-hundred feet long.

Galberon: Demon. Female. Petrious. Twelve feet tall. Explosives expert. Works with Marcus Blood.

Glaveroot: Demonic healing herb.

Glowerfine Path: Named for Sir Glowerfine, who unified all kingdoms of Phalon under one rule.

Gravelmole: A sightless creature of the Demonic Realm. The word is often used as an insult for when people cannot see something obvious.

Groddish: Phalonic vegetable. It's seriously gross. I'm not sure why people still bother eating them.

Hedda: Demon. Female. Balchen. Rank of Lieutenant in the Spider Horde. Leading a company of spiders stranded in the Human Realm.

Ivy Green: Human. Female. Six foot tall. Long brown hair. Exceptional speed. A trained nurse. Member of the Sugar House Wasps.

Kelly Green: Human. Male. Six foot tall. Short brown hair. Incredible reflexes. Works as an Emergency Medical Technician. Member of the Sugar House Wasps.

Kolan the Wraith: Torn apart by a spell as the Patriarch laid it upon a sword.

Laisuma: Fildoran. Female. Osamu's oldest sister. A fine dragon, respected and loved by all her peers.

Lord Dragon: Ruler of all dragons. Current title belongs to Slavadornectan.

Lucinda: Chief Healer of the Phalonians. On board the Moonship Gaeleon with the royal family.

Marcus Blood: The most successful and sought-after jewelry maker in the world. Pieces designed and made by him are worth millions.

Melferim: Once known as the Goddess of Snakes. A skilleck, with a human-like torso and snake tail. Lived during the time of the Second Incursion. Sister of the Patriarch and Aberdem. Mother of Corthas the Apprentice.

Melissa McConnell: Human. Female. Five feet, four inches tall. Short brown hair. Works at Smiths and volunteers at the library on weekends.

Mengodordum: The Ant, God of Insects.

Petrious: Demons with grey, nigh impenetrable skin, human-like in appearance.

Rownknife: (Roh-en-nife) A common flowering plant in the Demonic Realm with blade-like branches.

Sapphyril: A metal which is dark blue in color. Known for its affinity to magic. Anciently, it was often used in demonic weapons, though it is much rarer in modern times.

Sinewol: (Sine-e-wohl) "The blade forged twice." Originally forged by Kolan the Wraith. So much magic was poured into the blade the sapphyril became weak. The second time it was forged by the Patriarch. Designed to tear humans asunder without touching their flesh.

Snowchest: Phalonic term for shivers associated with fever.

Stone Battle: A popular game on Phalon for hundreds of years. Stone figures representing warriors combat one another in a display of skill and strategy.

Stonevale: Home of the Petrious. Under the dominion of Maxagagen.

The Warrior's Triune: The three weapons forged in answer to the request to create the most powerful weapon in existence. Corthas is the blacksmith primarily responsible for their design and forging.

The Well: An event of potent emotion-manipulating magic. The Well, founded in a being who is like-minded with the creator, forms an aura of magical energy which effects almost all beings within its corona. The effect corrodes the barrier between the being's baser emotions and their restraint, resulting in beings acting with more anger, hate, and lust.

Only those with an Ironsoul remain unaffected. The most recent Well was formed by Mr. Fingers in the Human Realm, specifically located in Bleakwood.

Tremanchen: Second smallest race of spiders. Approximately 8-10 feet tall.

Yadira: Demon. Female. Tremanchen. The medic—by coincidence, not by training—of the band of spiders trapped in the Human Realm.

Appendix A

Billy Blacksmith.

Quinn Blouin's
Notes on the Demonic Races.

=Demon Gods=

- little G.
- God is a title / level of power that they can earn.

→ Aldergaben. "The ~~Bat~~ God of Bats"
- Titles: Patriarch
  Master of Demonspells
  Traitor
- Died when performing The Blacksmith Ritual.
  (But who said "Mine" when I touched Anarchaisr?)

→ Aberdem "The God of Dragons"
- Titles: Human~~slayer~~
- Killed ~~billions~~ of humans during the Second Incursion.

→ Myserec "The Bull"
- Titles: "Maker of Ways"
- Probably responsible for laying the magical foundation
  that ~~allows~~ allows travel between ~~an~~ realms.

→ Geradutar - "The Child" ¿??
- Title: The Weeper ?
- (why don't we know ~~an~~ anything ???)

→ Odergon - "The Millipede" (oh, what the hell?)
- Title: With 70 hands and 70 hammers.
- Increases power by adding minds from volunteers.
  "Like adding sticks of RAM" - Greyson.

①

160

Billy Blacksmith

= Demidemons =

- Only 2 left. Thanks to Maxagagen
  Max - ~~ugh~~ uh - gae - gen

-> Maxagagen "The Consumer of Gods"
  - Title↗   - Demonhound. ~ 80 ft tall.
  - killed all other demidemons except Winged King

-> The Winged king.
  - Title: The ~~peat~~ Keeper of Kings.
  - 40 ft tall
  - Lost his mind when I beat Mr. Fingers.
    (But that doesn't make sense.
     Does it ?)

= Demon Royalty =

Only races. Others have kings too. "significant"

- Equivalent doesn't mean equivalent. It's just something
  you're familiar with
                              <- Animals ¬
                                          ↓

Race	Equivalent	Sovereign.
- Papabowa	bat	Currently, none.
Arietem	Ram	Greelor
Hebridick	4 horned sheep	Baaler
Skilleck	Snake	Saverous.
Javels	Panther	Silventh
Gilmoth	Rhino	Materion
Clemil	Wolf	Findel
Whollish	Polar bear	Unnuk
Swargill	Bird	Falmaloo
Petrious	Human-like	Grantin

②

Billy Blacksmith

Demon Royalty – CONTINUED

~~Animal~~

Race	Equivalent	Sovereign
Tanbel	Octopus	Squillard
Mar-Moncherim	Gargantuan Elephant.	Delmaia
Fimlu	Sharks	Fangerous.

Insects →

Race	Equivalent	Sovereign.
Haskelous	Beetles	Ahotepre.
Spiders	Nope.	Theron? (~~Ded Dead?~~)
Scaverous	Scorpion	Nakhiti
Sprites	None	Ravel
Badru	Praying Mantis	Skittle.
Ganetulous	Giant beetles.	Not sure.

Dragons →

Race	Equivalent	Sovereign
Kamoman	Komono dragon-ish	Toromane
Fildoran	NOT Japanese (But they are)	Hiamin Slavadornectar
Amerot	European (Game of Thrones)	"Lord of Dragons" rules all 3 kingdoms

③

Billy Blacksmith.

=All Races=
Quick Reference

BOOORING
STAY on your
OWN PAPER
ASHES!!

Race	Equivalent
Amerob	European dragon
Antel	Giant octopus. (100 ft long)
Ara-Aritem	Giant ram. (40 ft tall)
Arachnis.	Gargantuan spider (20 ft)
Arameous.	Spider-centaur
Arietem	Ram
Badru	Praying Mantis
Balchen	Large spider (13 ft)
Barcrien	Stick bugs. (That was the guy at the salt factory I thought was a tree-demon. OUH)
Blattodon	Cockroach (I KNEW THIS!)
Clemil	Wolf
Encherop	Leech
Fanderonts	Ant
Fangrach	Penguin
Fildoran	Japanese Dragon. (Like Osamu)
Finnlu	Sharks
Flanex	Fox
Flimpan	Hummingbird. (But 5ft tall)
Garantel	Gargantuan Octopus (200 - 400 ft)
Garetulous	Giant beetles (20 ft)
Garmiltus	Potato bug (150 ft long)
Garzim	Bee. (10 ft)
Gilmoth	Rhino. (But can be a rhino-dude Probably the guy that attacked Ashes)

④

163

Billy Blacksmith

=All Races=

... continued.

Gralboem — Frogs (50 ft tall) "Not aggressive, but very dangerous"

~~Grind~~

Gridnew — Crab

Harlepom — Eagle

Harrig — Hawk

Hasketous — Beetles

Hebridick — 4 horned sheep (What people think of as a "Normal" demon?)

Helminet — Orangutan

Javels — Panther (can also look human ish)

Kamoman — Kimono dragon

Kukobom — Kookaburra

Mar-Moncherim — Gargantuan elephant (60 ft)

Martimah — Elk

Minminet — Tiny orangutan

Moncherim — Elephant (30 ft tall)

Papabowa — Bat ← Seth says he is.

Petrious — Human-like | But so does Lilly. And they don't look alike

← Flame Monster DON'T CARE

Scaverous — "Small" scorpion. (little guys. Jerks. Not very strong)

Scolneps. — "Tiny" spiders. (2 ft tall)

Shadowlurk — Smallest spider (5 ft)

Shaderoc — Pandas

Skilleck — Snake (can be snake-centaur)

⑤

= All Races =

... still continued. Ugh

Skiverious	Giant scorpions (CRAP. These guys are giant TOO ??)
Sprites.	Big fairies. (Seth says call then that and they'll "cut off your face")
Swargill	Seagull (Like Celia)
Tentell	Octopuses. (AGAIN)
Terious.	Bull - Bull & actual bull centaur.
Tremarchen	Medium spider (8 ft)
Valomp	Vulture
Whollish	Polar bear (like eel normal polar bears weren't bad enough.)

- Not an exhaustive list -

⑥

Appendix B

For Queen Natalie. Found when one of the Fillmian assistants dropped a stack of parchments. She was exceedingly distressed as they were addressed to her Captain Gartell. This parchment was discovered only after the Fillmians had left the moonships and could not be returned to her.

Acknowledgements

*My face bloodied, my lip swollen,
I meet the eyes of my wife in the audience*

"I wub yoo."

About the Author

Born and raised in Australia, Ben Ireland is uniquely qualified to write about horrifying spiders and how much they would like to kill you. An award-winning writer of both Young Adult Urban Fantasy and Cyber-Horror, Ben received the Gold Quill 2017 for Billy Blacksmith: The Demonslayer from the League of Utah Writers. His other award-winning books include Billy Blacksmith: The Hellforged, The Ironsoul; the cyber-horror series – Kingdom City, and several short stories.

www.ingramcontent.com/pod-product-compliance
Lightning Source LLC
Chambersburg PA
CBHW051825170626
46807CB00003B/1029